# TREASURE HUNTED

# Treasure Hunted

by Cy Bishop

ISBN-13: 9798830464185

Imprint: Independently Published

With special thanks to:

God, my patient family, Google,

and Sonja Hutchinson and Jessica Dodson for all their help.

# Prologue

Easy prey. He walked steadily onward, his feet making no sound on the pavement. The same couldn't be said for the woman in front of him, who tottered drunkenly on her ankle-endangering stilettos. She'd parted ways with her friends, electing to wander solo through the parking lot toward the nearby park, most likely a shortcut back to the local college campus. She smelled delicious.

They entered the cover of the park, trees hiding them from prying eyes of potential witnesses. He increased his pace, but only slightly. It was a large park. There was no rush.

The woman swayed and staggered sideways a couple steps before regaining her forward momentum. Completely oblivious to his presence. She pawed at her purse, apparently searching for something, unaware of the items falling out and littering the ground along the trail.

He didn't have to look around to be sure they were alone. He smelled the friends still saying their farewells in the parking lot. A couple other drunks making their own stilted path home. A handful of people on the far end of the park working their way to their cars.

The nearest living being was a cat prowling the branches above. But even if it could speak, he got the impression it would applaud his actions and offer an intellectual critique of his methods rather than sound the alarm.

The woman tilted again. Straightened. Muttered to herself. Half of her hair fell loose from its style, brushing her shoulders. She pushed it back with irritated, jerky movements.

He smiled. Almost there. The bushes grew thick here, the dirt soft. There would be no evidence left when he finished. He followed only three meters behind her. Two meters. One.

He reached for her neck.

His fingers slowed. Instinct waned, dampened by disappointment. This was too easy. Too simple.

He changed his aim. Caught her shoulder. Turned her around to face him.

"Wha…?" she slurred, staring at him with alcohol-blurred eyes.

His smile returned. He knew what she saw.

It took a moment for her soused brain to process. He waited patiently. The anticipation sharpened his senses and drew saliva. Soon.

Her eyes widened.

There it was.

She screamed. Spun. Ran as best as she could.

Delicious.

He watched her, reveling in the moment, holding himself back to let the anticipation grow stronger.

She vanished into the bushes, still screaming.

A growl escaped his mouth as he lunged into the hunt.

Minutes later, he had nearly finished his feast when the other finally decided to show herself. He didn't bother to look up as she approached. He could sense her own desire to join him, but the kill was his. She didn't dare touch one bite.

She maintained a respectful distance. "I suppose you heard about the new discovery."

He didn't answer.

"And I'm sure you, of all of us, understand the implications."

He again didn't answer, but he knew exactly what she meant. He'd been contemplating the same matters himself.

She stepped closer and crouched to meet his eyes. "You must insert yourself into this. For all of us. This could change everything."

Of course it could. It would. He'd see to that.

Her gaze drifted to the last scraps of meat in front of him, but she respectfully looked away. He grabbed one of the bones and tossed it at her. She pounced, devouring it in a flash. When she looked at him again, her eyes held a knowing smile.

"You will do this," she said, sounding pleased. "Our people will rise once again and make this world ours."

CY BISHOP

# Chapter 1

Gina Gale slapped a mosquito against the papers in front of her, making a brown and red smear across her chicken-scratch notes. She scowled and scraped it away with one hand while the other wiped sweat off the back of her neck. Even her lightest cotton blouse wasn't enough to keep her cool in the South American jungle heat. If she was there for any other reason, she'd have packed up and returned home to moderate temperatures and air conditioning days ago. But she was closer to finding the Ruby of Ages than ever in her life, and she wasn't about to let a little sweltering, oppressive heat slow her down. Much.

The tent flap opened, admitting Dieter Grunewald. He yawned and eyed the books and notes spread out over the camp table in front of her. "You got an early start."

"Something like that," she mumbled, setting the stained notes aside and picking up a fresh page. She'd learned so much in the last week. She and Dieter had rushed down to this untamed corner near Chile's border as soon as Kaufman announced his discovery. A new cave filled with Mevoyan murals and writings. There hadn't been a new discovery in the years the two of them had been studying the language and culture together, and she couldn't pass up the chance to learn more.

In truth, even if there hadn't been some new clues to the ruby's location, she still would have come. The ancient, lost tribe had been her passion ever since Kaufman spoke at her university. She'd been a starry-eyed college girl, enraptured by his descriptions of their language. She hadn't known then what a jerk he was, a lesson she'd now learned time and again. The latest evidence was the deal he cut with the government to get exclusive access to the new discovery. He had reluctantly allowed a few others access—Gina and Dieter among them—but his team controlled which areas of the cave the others were allowed to see. They claimed it was because the off-limits areas were devoid of paintings and were being used as workstations for their studies, but she still couldn't shake the feeling they were deliberately hiding some of the murals for their own private study.

Dieter sat across from her. "You stayed up all night again, didn't you."

"I didn't mean to," she said. He was always on her case for the little things, like when she got so caught up in the work she forgot to eat or sleep. "Some guy from Kaufman's team… I think his name's Shane? He said he wanted to meet me last night near the cave. He made it sound urgent, but he never showed. I guess I got caught up in studying after that."

"Shane?" Tad Malone said as he wandered into the tent. He plopped into the last free chair. "Heard he was in an accident in the cave last night. Some rockslide or whatever."

Gina looked up, startled. "Is he okay?"

"Nah, they had to dig his body out. All mangled and crap."

She stared in shock, but he seemed unimpressed. He flicked a mosquito off his shoulder. "Not like it matters much. Kaufman's team is way ahead of you guys."

She pulled herself back together. "How would you possibly know that?"

"I was chatting with them this morning. Told 'em what you figured out, and they just laughed. They got that stuff ages ago." He stretched. "I found a pretty cheap flight back home that leaves tomorrow morning. I should get our tickets ordered before they're all booked."

Dieter gave the younger man a frown. "That's a bit premature."

Tad shrugged. "Whatever."

Gina returned her attention to the pages in front of her, picking up one of the pictures she'd taken of the cave murals. They shouldn't have brought Tad along. He'd been assigned as their assistant for college credit, but he'd gone out of his way to make it obvious he had no interest in what they were doing. "Could you get the fifth and sixth research journals out of the case, please?"

"Sure," Tad said, putting his feet up and turning on his tablet computer. "Right on it."

She sighed and returned her attention to the picture.

Dieter walked around the table and hovered over her shoulder. "You've got the translation on that symbol wrong. It's more like 'fly' than 'run' in this context."

"Thanks." She corrected her notes. While Kaufman's team was more of a one-man show, with Kaufman as the star translator and the others as mere assistants, she and Dieter had always been a team. She was better at identifying the symbols and their technical, precise translations, while Dieter was far stronger at understanding the nuance of the language, the contextual cues and idioms. By working together, they managed to get fairly accurate translations every time.

"Hey," Tad said. "Looks like they finally caught that Ondier that's been killing hikers around those Colorado mountains."

Gina looked up, once again startled.

"Good for them," Dieter said.

"There was an Ondier?" she asked, finally finding her voice. "I thought those were all gone. I mean, isn't that why we have Liberation Day? To celebrate the final battle that wiped them out decades ago?" A nervous chuckle escaped her. "If there are still Ondier around, then why do we get a day off every October ninth?"

Tad laughed. "Duh, of course there are still some out there. You think Liberation Day wiped them all out?" He laughed harder. "Right, and they also came to Earth through a magic window in the sky. I suppose you believe in the tooth fairy, too?"

She frowned at him.

Dieter cleared his throat. "The battle on Liberation Day eliminated enough of those monsters to prevent their population from ever recovering. They may not be entirely extinct yet, but there are so few remaining, they might as well be."

"So you better watch out, 'cause they're still out there," Tad said, smirking at Gina. He raised his arms and waved his fingers like he was trying to frighten a small child. "I could be one in disguise! If you aren't careful, I'll turn into my animal form and gobble you up! OoooOoo!"

Dieter sighed. "That's enough, Tad."

He grinned and went back to his tablet.

Dieter picked up one of the other pictures and made a few notes. "Did your all-nighter provide any new information? Nailed down the location of the cavern yet?"

"No such luck." She flipped back through her scrawled notes and found a few of them illegible even to her. "I got a few more clues about what we can expect to find in the cave, though. It talks about water that poisons any who touch it, making them long for more until they plunge in and are killed. That could be describing the central pool where the ruby is supposed to be, or it could be one of the surrounding traps."

"If the ruby is even in the pool," Tad said unhelpfully.

"We have to assume it is," she said, trying to keep her tone civil. He was right, though. Spanish explorers had found the ruby centuries ago, if an ancient parchment was to be believed. It was a message sent to their king from their ship, the *Corredor*, claiming that they had located the ruby in a cavern and were returning home with it. The message arrived intact. The ship never did.

Most scholars believed that the remnants of the Mevoyan people had attacked the ship and returned the ruby to its original place, though Mevoyan writings claimed that the power of the ruby had caused the sky to open and the ocean to rise against the ship, carrying it back into the cavern and destroying the sailors as punishment for their theft.

She wished yet again that she could speak to those Mevoyans, to learn more about what they had actually seen and done. But inter-tribal warfare had all but wiped out the Mevoyan people after that. The few who remained today had little to no understanding of their ancient language and culture.

The tent flap opened once more. Lettie Harrington poked her head in, looking as perky as ever in her Lara Croft-style outfit. "Good, you're all here. You better come quick."

Gina stood and followed her friend through their small camp toward the cave, Dieter right behind her. Tad dragged his feet, still focused on his tablet. At least Lettie was happy to be there, helping them. She'd been Gina's best friend since high school, always exuberant and eager to try new things. Her latest hobby had been archeology, thanks to an obsession with a young Harrison Ford and the latest Lara Croft video games, which had inspired her to join Gina and Dieter in their studies. If it wasn't for the fact that her father's parenting style amounted to writing blank checks to finance his daughter's string of hobbies, they wouldn't have even made it this far.

Kaufman, called 'Frahnk' by his team, stood in front of the cave with an important look on his face and a laptop facing him, web cam running. Several members of his team clustered behind him, echoing his expression.

Gina sighed. "Another press conference?"

"I think they've got something this time," Lettie whispered.

Gina folded her arms and waited.

Kaufman glanced her way. A smug smile crossed his face before he resumed speaking to the camera. "And I am most pleased to announce that we have discovered the precise location of the Ruby of Ages. I expect that my team will have recovered this priceless artifact by the end of the month, at the latest."

Her eyes widened. He'd already figured it out? How?

He continued talking, growing more insufferably smug with each sentence, but it was mostly meaningless bluster. His assistants showed images of murals and writings to the camera to illustrate his speech.

"And in this image, we discovered the key landmarks which will lead us to the cavern," Kaufman concluded, pointing to the last picture. "This symbol tells us that we are to 'fly,' or travel, several miles east of a certain landmark, and the cavern will be found there. We will remain in close contact, as I know you all back at home will be eager to see our progress. No questions at this time, but you are welcome to email them to me, as always."

One of his assistants terminated the connection. Kaufman shot Gina another smug smile, then directed his team in getting their gear together.

"Guess I'm booking those tickets after all," Tad said.

"They found it?" Lettie asked, looking wounded.

"Apparently," Dieter said.

Gina didn't speak. Her brain was working overtime, reviewing the images Kaufman's team had shown. Most of them had been familiar, but the last one…

She straightened and walked over to Kaufman. "Congratulations on your find."

His smile reached the pinnacle of smugness. "You made a nice effort, Miss Gale, but I'm afraid you just weren't up to par with the work required."

"That last image was interesting," she continued, ignoring his jab. "I don't think I'd seen it, even though you said we had access to all the writings in the cave."

"Well, there are some benefits to having an exclusivity deal with the government."

She'd been right. He'd kept something hidden from them. No wonder they hadn't been making any progress. "Well, now that you've gotten what you need from those paintings, may we have access to them?"

"So you can come chasing on our tails? No, thank you. You're just going to have to live with the knowledge that you are only second best."

Something from the image kept bothering her. But it was only a hunch. Maybe she shouldn't bother.

She glanced back at the disappointed look at Lettie's face, the frown on Dieter's. No. It was worth trying. "How about a deal?"

Kaufman raised an eyebrow.

"We promise not to follow you. In fact, we won't even set one toe in the cave where you go. In exchange, you let us see the off-limits sections of this cave. And the next time we beat you somewhere important, the same rule applies. You aren't allowed in."

He frowned for a moment, then burst out laughing. "You think you'd ever find anything before me? Sure. It's a deal."

Gina turned to the cave, once again ignoring his jabs. "Tell your goons to let us through, then."

Still laughing, he spoke into his radio as he walked away.

Dieter came to Gina's side as she entered the cave. He spoke quietly. "You saw something he missed."

Her study partner had always been perceptive. "I think he mistranslated something. I need to double-check, though. Tad, go grab the camera and a new journal."

"Why me?"

Dieter gave him a look.

He sighed in exasperation and wandered back toward their camp.

"You think we'll find something?" Lettie asked, hope cautiously buoyed.

"Maybe. We'll see."

When they reached the off-limits area, Kaufman's assistant rolled her eyes before stepping aside to let them through. A narrowed tunnel twisted its way deeper into the mountainside, then finally opened up into a wider space. Sure enough, paintings and writings covered the walls.

"And that would be why we weren't getting anywhere," Dieter said.

"We will now."

"Yay!" Lettie said.

Gina and Dieter worked their way around the room together, translating as quickly as they could. When Tad joined them, Gina took pictures of every square inch while Dieter dictated their translations for Tad to copy down. Lettie bounced around, examining every stalactite with the seriousness of a brain surgeon.

"Here it is," Gina said, taking another photo. It was the section of writing Kaufman claimed revealed the location. She smiled as she studied the symbols. She'd been right.

"What'd you find?" Dieter asked.

She glanced around. She couldn't see any of Kaufman's team lurking nearby, but that didn't mean they couldn't be listening. "Come on. Let's get this back to the camp."

Once in the privacy of their own tent, Gina showed Dieter the pictures she'd taken of the section in question. "He was right that he found the key landmark. See this image? That looks exactly like Pájaro Rojo."

Lettie squinted at the image. "Pa-what?"

"It means 'red rock.' It's a local landmark," Gina explained. She pointed to the symbol Kaufman had identified as 'fly.' "This. He thought it meant fly, as in traveling in a straight direction. But this word is more like 'soar,' or in this case, 'float.' As in, a downward direction."

Dieter stared, then understanding lit up his eyes. "Kaufman's going the wrong way."

"For reals?" Tad asked, looking surprised that Gina had figured out something Kaufman had missed.

"We're going to find it!" Lettie squealed.

"Pájaro Rojo is near a crevasse, if I recall correctly," Gina said, flipping through notes as she talked. "That's where we should find the cave entrance."

Dieter grinned. "And you just made a deal to guarantee that he can't follow us in there, even if he figures out his mistake."

"As long as we get in there first." Gina looked at Lettie. "Um, we'll need to hire some extra help for this part. And we'll need some supplies."

"On it." Lettie pulled out her mobile phone and activated the speed-dial for her father.

Gina looked over the pages in front of her, her smile spreading by the moment. They'd finally found it.

# Chapter 2

Gina gathered the last of her things into her aluminum-frame backpack. She could have just used her old bag, but Lettie had insisted that if they were going to undertake an archeological expedition, then they had to do it right. And by 'right,' she meant expensive. Top-quality gear, the latest innovations, and the best in the field hired to help them. Thankfully, her father's money worked fast, and it had only taken a few days to pull everything together.

Gina hardly recognized half of the things she was loading into her own bag. A high-end sleeping bag instead of the patched flannel one she'd used since her father took her on camping trips at eight years of age. A shiny first aid kit instead of her Altoids tin of Bandaids and antibiotic ointment. Even the camera was new, a fancy model designed to function well in low-light situations. And, given that the cave system most likely opened to the ocean on the other end, Lettie had made sure to get a fully waterproof model. All those items in the pack, along with a lantern, a headlamp, and dozens of protein bars and ready-to-eat camp meals, barely left enough room for two books.

She looked back over her collection of research in dismay. She'd collected and copied notes and images from their findings about the ruby into one journal, so that was obviously the first choice. But now she had to choose from all her books and only bring one more?

Tad wandered in, fiddling with his own pack. The frame stuck up above his head in a way that looked professional on the REI website but comical on him. "We going or what?"

Gina cringed internally. She'd meant to have Dieter address this. "Um, I thought, you know, the expedition is going to be dangerous, and we don't even know how long it'll take..."

He continued fumbling with his straps.

"I mean, it could take days. Or more. We don't know. So, since you were pretty eager to head back home, and since we won't have as many books along for you to help us find our notes in, this would be a good time for you to... you know..."

He raised one eyebrow in her general direction, but still didn't look her way.

She took a deep breath and got it all out in one rush. "A good time for you to go. We'll sign off on your credits and everything. I, um, we just thought it'd be better this way. For you."

He finally got the buckle to latch properly and laughed. "I didn't waste all that time listening to you eggheads just to skip out when there's finally a chance something exciting might happen."

Her heart sank at the unexpected turn. She'd thought he would jump on the chance to split. "You really believe we got it right, then?"

"Naw, not really. If you did, cool, I get to be there to find that hunk of rock. If you didn't, I get to be there to watch you crash and burn." He whistled a falling rocket sound. "Should be a good show either way."

A few sharp words sprang to Gina's tongue, but she couldn't find it in herself to get them any further than that.

The tent flap opened and admitted Dieter. "All set?"

"I can only choose one more book." Her tone sounded whinier than she'd intended. "I mean, I don't know exactly what we'll find in those caves, so I'm not sure which texts will be the most useful."

Dieter crossed to the collection and poked through a couple of them. "I thought we had all of the information we needed in your journal."

"Yeah, but the full descriptions and reviews are in these." She joined him and grabbed a book, then another. "Should we take the one from the second dig site with the descriptions of the maze? Or maybe the general book with their ritual practices? That could be handy. But maybe we should—"

His hand landed on her hastily gathered stack of books, stopping her before she snatched another. "You know the full descriptions and reviews. You know all the footnotes and scholarly disagreements and articles and debates. Quit worrying."

"But—"

He held up the last book she'd grabbed, keeping the cover shut. "What's on page 59, about halfway down the page?"

She glanced at the title and thought for a second. "That's the discussion on their purification rituals, but I don't see how that…" The look on his face told her he'd made his point. It took her a moment longer to get it. She made a face at him. "I get it. You don't think we need them. But I still have space for one more, and I don't know which one." She gave him a pleading look. "You have extra space, right?"

He shook his head. "My pack's full."

"Don't look at me," Tad said preemptively.

Gina sighed and turned back to the books, still at a loss.

"There will be more writings within the caves, won't there?" Dieter asked.

"Sure. This would be one of their sacred places. They'd have included some writings in the design."

"Then why not bring a blank notebook?" Dieter crossed to the other trunk and tossed a blank book her way. "We'll need to copy down the translations as we go."

Why hadn't she thought of that? She suddenly felt ridiculous. "Right. Sorry. I should've—"

The pack twisted on one strap as she tried to cram the notebook into the miniscule space left. She lost her grip, and it crashed to the dirt floor, spilling supplies.

She stamped her foot. "Fudgesicles!"

Tad laughed out loud. "Fudgesicles? I'm so tweeting that."

Gina exhaled and crouched to gather her items, doing her best to ignore Tad and her burning cheeks.

Dieter knelt beside her to help. "This is a big day for us. It's okay to be a little flustered."

The embarrassment faded in the light of his words. "All these years of studying and searching," she said, unable to keep from smiling.

He returned her grin. "Finally coming to fruition."

Lettie breezed in, looking half Lara Croft and half camping magazine model. "All set?"

"Just about." Gina finished restoring order to her pack and stood. "Was there any extra room for more of the books?"

Her friend looked surprised. "I thought you just needed that one journal."

"It'd be better if I could bring more. There are going to be a lot of traps in there, and the more notes we have, the better we'll be able to make our way through them."

"Oh!" Lettie's eyes gleamed. "Like maybe the ruby will be on a pedestal, and if you take it off, it'll release a pressure plate, and then a big rock will fall down from the ceiling, and—"

"Something to that effect," Dieter said. He sounded amused.

"It must've been really special to the Mevoyans, if they put all those traps around," Lettie mused.

"According to the writings, it was considered the heart of the people and was revered as having great powers." Gina's mind drifted back through her studies as she recited. "It pulses with the souls of the righteous, and when called upon, it will melt the sky and shape the oceans."

Lettie's eyes went wide. "Like it did with the Spanish explorers, right? So it really has powers like that?"

"No." Gina chuckled, snapping out of her scholarly haze. "Of course not. The Spanish explorers were most likely the unfortunate victims of a hurricane that happened to drive their ship back toward the cave they'd left. It only fueled the Mevoyan people's beliefs in the ruby's powers, though. But it's just a ruby. A really, really, really big ruby."

A new gleam sparked in Lettie's eyes. "How big?"

"You have not paid much attention as we studied," Dieter said.

Lettie pouted. "You guys were just looking at pictures and books. I was waiting for the cave parts."

"The picture and book parts are what lead to the cave parts," Dieter said. "To answer your question, the writings describe it as larger than a grown man's brain."

"Wow," Lettie breathed, then she wrinkled her nose. "Yuck."

"Anyway, what do you think?" Gina tried to steer the conversation back to the original topic. "Is there room for more books?"

Lettie shook her head. "Sorry. You should've said something to me sooner. I hired a guy to put together a work crew to carry everything we'll need, and I had to give him an exact weight of everything we'd be carrying. If I'd known, I'd have told him about the books, too, but…"

"It will be fine," Dieter said. He gave Gina a confident look that she couldn't quite share. "The journal will be enough."

"So," Tad said, sounding a mix between annoyed and bored. "We going or what?"

Lettie turned questioning eyes on Gina and Dieter.

Dieter adjusted his pack. He actually did look more like the professional in the REI ads. "Yes. We're going."

It took a few hours to ride in Lettie's mauve Jeep over pitted dirt roads, but they finally reached Pájaro Rojo. The rust-toned rock jutted skyward only a few miles from the ocean. The deep crevasse they would soon enter sank into the ground, starting near the base of the landmark.

A small crowd had already gathered near the rock, a mass of chatting and pack adjusting. Gina stared with wide eyes. There had to be at least fifteen people there. "Are they all here for our team?"

"Yup, all ours!" Lettie checked her lipstick in the rearview mirror before turning off the Jeep and climbing out.

Gina kept staring as Lettie rushed through a flurry of introductions and fielded several last-minute questions. She hadn't expected quite so many people. Tad's comment about crashing and burning rang through her ears. It would've been one thing to do so with a small, quiet group. But if she was wrong, and it turned out they'd dragged all these people here for nothing…

She shook her head and climbed out of the Jeep on legs that only shook a little. She was letting her pride get ahead of her. If she'd made a mistake, then she'd made a mistake. They'd just try again, and these people would have gotten a couple days' paid vacation in South America. No harm done except to her reputation, and she could get over that easily enough. It wasn't like anyone knew or cared who she was, anyway.

Besides, she wasn't wrong. She was sure of it.

She tried to return her focus to the people she was supposed to be getting to know, but introductions had already passed. Most of the gathered people seemed to be a motley gang of burly men and women in work boots and grubby shirts, laughing coarsely and shouting nicknames back and forth. The work crew, she presumed.

She spotted lanky man who looked barely out of high school standing almost a full head taller than anyone else. Their guide, Will Young. From what Lettie had gushed about him, in addition to being a 'serious hottie,' he was some sort of spelunking prodigy who'd been exploring caves since he was only a kid.

Near him was a matronly black woman arguing with a muscular, well-tattooed man over a pack of Doritos. The doctor, Gina recalled. Dr. Cheyenne Richards, a doctor and nutrition expert. Just in case, Lettie had said. Accidents happen. Gina could only hope the woman's skills wouldn't be needed. A clean-cut man stood next to her, looking emphatically bored.

"You can leave them in the Jeep," Dr. Richards said, pointing as if directing a child. "But I won't have any of that junk food along here. You'll dehydrate in a day eating that garbage."

"I didn't sign on to have my food dictated to me," Tattoos growled.

Gina eyed the ink covering his arms. He must be one of the members of the work crew. The leader, perhaps? Part of her hoped not. Even if the tattoos didn't make him look like they'd pulled him out of some back alley to be here, there was something in his dark scowl that Gina didn't like.

"Technically, since they hired a nutritionist, you did," the doctor said. "Put it away."

Tattoos stuck a beefy finger in the smaller woman's face. Somehow, she still looked more intimidating than he did, even with his hostile pose. "Look here, lady—"

"Petty!" A bald man with a goatee strode over. He was only slightly smaller than the other man, but his muscles seemed to fit his frame better. "You got a problem?"

Petty sized up the other man. "Lady says I can't have my chips."

"Then you can't have your chips." The man's tone dared Petty to question him.

The larger man seemed to consider doing just that, but finally scowled and stormed back toward a gritty Jeep a few yards away, griping all the way.

"Apologies, ma'am," the man said, giving Dr. Richards a polite nod. "If any of my grunts give you any more grief, tell 'em Owen'll have the hide of any man or woman who crosses you."

"Thank you." The doctor eyed his pack. "You aren't smuggling any rot in with you, are you?"

"Wouldn't dream of it," Owen said, mushing a hand at his pocket. Gina caught a glimpse of a candy wrapper before it vanished under his hand.

"Good."

Owen caught Gina's look and gave her a wink before marching off to holler at a few other people in the work crew.

So he was the leader of the crew. She found herself relieved. He seemed like he'd keep things under control.

"You," the bored man said, pulling her attention back. "You're one of the translators, right? In charge?"

Gina blinked at him, searching her mind. She knew he was there as Dr. Richards' assistant, but couldn't quite remember his name. She thought Lettie had said something about 'Burke,' but she couldn't recall if that was a first or last name.

"Well?" Burke asked, impatience adding an edge to the word.

"Yes," she blurted. "Sorry. Yes, I'm one of the translators."

"What's that guy doing here?" He jerked a thumb toward Will.

Gina glanced at Will, not quite sure she understood the question. "He's an expert on caves. He's going to help guide us—"

"Expert? I heard of this kid. High-school dropout, no formal training at all." Burke folded his arms and turned his glare from Will to her. "We're supposed to be following some clown who couldn't even finish school?"

"No worries," Will said as he ambled over to Gina's side.

She cringed inside. She hadn't realized he'd be able to hear Burke's words over the background din of workers.

But Will only grinned and continued, a soft Australian accent adding playfulness to his voice. "I can't do algebra to save my life, mate, but you put me underground with a rope and my GPS," he patted a yellow electronic device hanging from his belt, "and no matter how deep it is, I'll find the safest way back to surface before you can say, 'Gee, I'm glad my guide knows what he's doing.'" He shrugged. "I just know caves."

"I'd rather have someone who 'just knows caves' because he's been trained," Burke said.

"Enough of that." Dr. Richards gave him a severe look. "If Miss Harrington felt he was the best fit to guide us, then we'll trust her judgment. Go make sure they've packed enough water."

Burke gave Will one last glare but turned and walked away.

"So you're the genius Lettie couldn't stop talking about?" Will asked, shaking Gina's hand before she really knew what was happening. "It's a pleasure."

"Yes," she said. "I mean, no, I'm not a genius. I've just studied—"

"A total genius," Lettie said, appearing at Gina's side and draping an arm over her shoulders. "She's the one who figured out where the ruby really is, unlike that jerk Kaufman." She cast a sly look at Will. "Guess you two have a lot in common, huh? The so-called experts don't think much of you, but you're both a lot better at what you do than any of them."

Gina's cheeks burned furiously. She tried to take a step backwards, but her friend's arm kept her from moving. "I'm sure you'll do a great job," she managed to mumble. "Nice to meet you."

"Thanks," Will said as she squirmed free and scurried away.

Lettie followed close behind. "Did I call it or what? Isn't he too cute? And that accent!" She fanned herself.

"So go flirt with him." Gina brushed imaginary dust off her shirt to cover her embarrassment. It was like middle school all over again, her friends trying to push romances on her that she had no interest in. Though she had to admit, Lettie was right. He was awfully cute.

Lettie feigned innocence. "I'm just saying, that's all."

Gina was already scanning the crowd. There was one person she hadn't seen yet. She'd written to the Mevoyan Cultural Association to tell them of her plans to search for the ruby and ask if they wished to send along a representative of their people. She hadn't expected any response, since the association had been working with Kaufman. She'd been delighted when she got an answer telling her they'd be sending a man named Savion to join her expedition. She couldn't wait to meet a living, breathing representative of the people she'd spent so many years studying. But he didn't seem to have arrived yet.

A low rumble announced the arrival of several more Jeeps. Gina turned, hoping to see the Mevoyan representative, but instead found Kaufman scowling at her.

"I thought we had a deal," he said, eying her group.

She hadn't expected him to be here. She'd thought his team had started their expedition long before now.

"You're only starting now?" Dieter raised an eyebrow. "Let me guess. You had to wait for satellites to reposition so your every brilliant move could be captured for the people back home."

Kaufman gave Dieter a look. "As I'm sure you're aware, it takes time to prepare a proper expedition. But that's beside the point. You shouldn't be here at all."

"We're still keeping the deal," Gina blurted. She had to make sure Kaufman didn't figure out the real reason they were there. "I just… I wanted to get a closer look at Pájaro Rojo. In case there were any carvings in it."

Kaufman stared at her, still frowning.

She searched her mind, trying to come up with something, anything she could say that would convince him they were harmless. She heard a few people shifting behind her and tensed up. The people Lettie had hired knew they were going after the ruby, and might not realize the importance of keeping their goal from Kaufman. What if one of them said something?

"It seems reasonable enough that if the Mevoyan writings mentioned this particular landmark, they may have had a camp or even a village near here at one point," Dieter said. "We simply wish to scout the area and see if we might find another cave."

Kaufman's frown persisted, but then he laughed. "Sure. You go ahead and do that. I'm sure you'll find some fantastic arrowheads to show off while I bring home the Ruby of Ages." Still smirking, he turned and walked away, shouting orders to his team as he went.

Gina exhaled in relief and gave Dieter a grateful smile for his save.

Doctor Richards stepped closer. "Excuse me. I was under the impression that we—"

"We are," Dieter said. "But he doesn't need to know that."

She smiled. "I see."

Will stretched in a way that would make a yoga expert jealous. "He's after the same thing, huh?"

"Shouldn't we start moving then?" Burke asked, glancing at Kaufman's team. "Or is the plan to sit around while they get to it first?"

Gina jumped at his voice. She hadn't heard him return from checking the supplies. Wishing he'd lower his voice, she spoke quietly and hoped he'd get the hint. "He's going a different direction than we are." At his confused frown, she explained further. "He thinks the ruby will be in a cave to the east, but it will actually be down in the crevasse."

"What makes you so sure you got it right and he got it wrong?" Burke pressed. "Maybe this is just a waste of time."

"Tell me about it," Tad muttered.

"We're fairly certain," Dieter said. "And you're getting paid if we find it or not, so I'm not sure why you're concerned."

Burke shot a scowl in his direction but stopped talking.

"Besides, it's going to be an adventure either way." Lettie brushed off her khaki shorts. "I can't believe I'm actually going to search a cave for an artifact!"

"Hey!" Kaufman called, drawing their attention. He stood with his team, about to set out. He waved. "Good luck finding those arrowheads!" With that, his group set out, laughing and high-fiving each other.

"Kind of a dick, isn't he," Burke said.

"I wouldn't necessarily say that." Gina felt her cheeks warm at the crude language.

"I would," Dieter said.

Burke nodded as if thinking the matter over. "Let's make him eat his words." He turned toward the crevasse.

Dieter stopped him. "We should wait until they're a distance away. I don't want them seeing us descend and realize that we figured out something they didn't."

"Besides, we're still waiting on one more," Gina added, looking around. Nothing but dank jungle behind them, giving way to lower shrubs and ferns around where they stood. No sounds but the steady ruckus of birds and buzzing of mosquitos she'd gotten used to in the last few days. Where could he be?

"In retrospect, I'm glad they didn't get an earlier start," Dieter mused. "He might have figured out he had the wrong place and rechecked his translations before we had a chance to get here."

"Good point." Gina's answer was distracted; she still searched for signs of their last party member.

A man spoke behind her, his voice heavily accented. "I am sorry I am late."

She jumped a mile and turned. And looked up. And up. A wall of earth-skinned man stood behind her, his face chiseled in a severe expression. She stumbled back a few steps. Where had he come from?

Dieter recovered first. "Dieter Grunewald. I'm guessing you're here to represent the Mevoyan people."

"Savion." He shook Dieter's hand. "We are ready to go?"

Gina managed to find her voice again and held out her hand to shake. "I'm Gina. Um, Gale. Gina Gale. And I must say, I am so honored to meet you. I've been studying the Mevoyan language and culture for—"

"Which way do we go?" Savion adjusted the rough leather pack on his back. His clothes looked more modern than she'd expected, a cotton short-sleeved shirt and thick cargo pants. He even wore dark hiking boots.

"I guess we're ready to get started?" Will asked, glancing at Lettie.

Lettie looked at Gina and Dieter.

Dieter checked the east and nodded. "Looks like Kaufman's team is far enough away."

Will walked over to the crevasse, where the work crew had already set up ropes for their descent. "Let's go, then."

Savion strode over to join Will, leaving Gina standing with her hand still extended.

"Man of few words, it seems," Dieter said. He almost sounded amused.

She exhaled and dropped her hand. That hadn't quite gone as she'd hoped. But part of her was a bit relieved. As awed as she might be standing in the presence of the living representative of her studies, he seemed… scary. Though she felt somewhat childish admitting that, even to herself.

"Anything in particular we should watch for?" Will asked as he helped Lettie with her climbing harness.

Gina dug into her pack and pulled out her journal. "There isn't much to indicate what order we'll find things. We should find a Room of Closure before a Room of Safety, and somewhere in there we'll encounter a labyrinth that I have directions for, but I'm not sure if those will be first, last, or somewhere in the middle."

"A Room of Closure? What the heck is that supposed to mean?" Burke asked.

"Probably a sealed room." Speaking on her subject of expertise helped Gina relax. "We'll have to figure out how to get through it once we're there. According to the writings, the ruby itself will be inside a pool in a great cavern, but it's hard to say for sure if that's true now. The Spanish ship most likely crashed near the exit of the cave system, so unless the pool is near the exit, then the ruby is probably a bit further along."

"In a pool?" Lettie sounded disappointed. "I thought there'd be some sort of trap."

"Like a pedestal with a pressure plate," Tad said under his breath.

"According to the writings, the pool could be toxic," Dieter said.

"Really?" Lettie grinned.

Gina shook her head at her friend's adventure-lust. She peered over the edge of the crevasse, placing one hand against a nearby tree for balance. It ran long and narrow, so narrow that it looked like they'd be able to touch both sides at once at about three yards down. She couldn't see the bottom from where she stood. A wave of nausea swept over her.

She straightened to see Savion staring at her. "Oh. Hi." She pushed the nausea aside and summoned her courage. "I was saying before, I've been studying your history ever since—"

He flung his hand.

She only had time to see a glint of metal and hear a thudding sound as the blade shot past her ear and hit the tree behind her.

Her whole body locked up in terror.

# Chapter 3

Savion stepped forward. Reached past her. Pulled the knife free.

A snake dangled from the blade briefly before dropping free against the tree with a soft thump.

Lettie let out a squeak.

Gina couldn't even manage that much.

"Fer-de-Lance. Those snakes are poisonous," Doctor Richards said, her tone professional. "Were you bitten? I brought anti-venom."

Savion wiped the small knife off on the grass, then it disappeared somewhere in his clothes. "No."

Gina finally recovered enough to scurry a few steps away. A long, tan snake dangled limply from higher branches, a smear of blood marking where the knife had pinned its head to the tree.

Dieter put a hand on her shoulder, almost making her jump again. "You all right?"

She swallowed and forced herself to speak as steadily as possible. "Fine." She glanced at Savion. "Thank you."

He didn't answer, already connecting his harness in preparation to descend along with Lettie, Will, and the first half of the work crew.

Right. Man of few words. She took a deep breath and shook off the last of the tremors. She'd have to work up some tougher reflexes. No telling exactly what they'd be facing in the caves, but it was likely to be at least that dangerous. She'd have to be ready for that so she wouldn't lock up like a wimp next time.

"Niiice," one of the workers drawled.

Gina looked over, glad for a distraction. The woman was the largest woman Gina had ever seen without being overweight. Broad shoulders, short-cropped hair, and bigger biceps than half the men there. She was casting a smirk in Lettie's direction. "We got us our own personal Lara Croft. Cute."

Petty snickered and elbowed the woman. "Good one, Lich."

"Thanks," Lettie chirped brightly, the sarcasm passing right over her head. She smoothed her khaki shorts under the harness. "I just love those games, don't you?"

"Sure. Play them all the time," Lich said, still smirking.

"Me, too!"

"Bug off," one of the other workers said. He gave Lich and Petty the stink eye.

Lich snorted but returned her attention to the ropes in front of her.

Lettie looked confused.

The other worker, a hefty man with the kind of stubble that made him look like an old country lumberjack rather than a grubby guy who didn't shave, gave her a friendly smile. "I'm Jake. Don't worry about them; they're just being dumb. Need any help?"

"I think I've got it," Lettie said, returning the smile. "Thanks."

He saluted and moved on to help a wiry man, the smallest worker on the crew, with his harness.

Lettie bounced on her toes and peeked over the edge. "Isn't this exciting?"

Gina nodded, though glancing in the same direction as her friend sent her stomach into a new twist. She swallowed it back and stared ahead instead, taking deep breaths. It was just a little climb down. That was all. Then they'd be safe in the caves.

She almost laughed at herself. Safe in the trap-laden caves. It's all relative.

Will gave the first group one last check. "Looks good." He tilted his face toward Gina and Dieter. "You two want in on the first group here?"

"No," Gina blurted before she could control her response.

Petty snorted and earned an elbow from Jake.

"I'll…" Dieter glanced at her with an inscrutable look, as if measuring her. "I'll wait for the next one, thank you."

Will bobbed his head and set to coaching the group.

Gina chewed a hangnail and missed most of what he said. The next thing she knew, the group climbed over the side of the ledge and began rappelling down.

"Guess we'll know soon if you got it right," Tad said, leaning over the edge.

She wished he wouldn't stand so close without a harness keeping him secure.

"Indeed," Dieter said in a dismissive tone. He faced Gina. "You're ready for this?"

She couldn't take her eyes off the edge in front of her. "It's what I've been studying all this time. The culture, that is. Not the ruby, specifically. But I've studied the ruby, too. And…" She was babbling, and she knew it. She shut her mouth.

"You'll do fine," he promised.

"Gina!" Lettie shouted from below. "Will says he sees a cave entrance!"

Excitement pushed the fear to the background. She was right. They'd found it.

"A cave," Tad said. "Doesn't mean it's the right cave."

"We'll find out soon enough," Dieter said. He handed Gina a harness. "Know how to use one of these?"

She turned it over three times before finding the top. It looked like a cross between a diaper and a thong. "Um…"

"I can help," Owen offered.

"We have it, thank you," Dieter said. He coached Gina through the process of getting all the straps and buckles in place. By the time they finished, she had to stand at a slight crouch.

"It'll help you rappel easier," Dieter told her. "Just lean back and let the ropes do the work."

Lean back? She looked down the steep drop and fought off another wave of nausea. "What happens if you lean in?"

Dieter laughed and shook his head. "Don't worry. It's not too far down. You'll be there before you know it." He hooked her harness onto one of the ropes. He directed her hands and gave her the last few directions that she barely heard.

She closed her eyes. She could do this.

She peeked down again.

No, she couldn't.

Gina gritted her teeth. This was stupid. She was this close to the greatest archeological find of the century, and she was letting a little cliff get in her way. A little sheer, deadly cliff.

Doctor Richards attached to the rope next to her and patted her shoulder. "We'll go together. On the count of three."

She squared her shoulders as the doctor steadily counted. Closed her eyes again.

"Three!"

Gina squashed every self-preservative instinct inside her and jumped.

The rope hummed as it whizzed through the connections on her harness, then her feet hit solid rock.

She opened her eyes. She'd done it? Sure enough, she crouched against the side of the crevasse, the rope supporting her weight.

"Good," Doctor Richards beamed. "Again."

With the doctor's coaching, Gina managed to work her way down. They had to lean in tightly at the narrow point, but the other side gapped back outward from there, creating more space. She peeked down and quickly looked away, taking deep breaths. She'd expected to see a clear bottom to the crevasse by now, but it only plunged deeper and deeper below her. She clenched her eyes tight and took another deep breath.

"Over here!" Lettie called. Her friend stood on a ledge on the opposite wall with a wide cave entrance behind her. "We found it! Isn't this awesome?"

Gina eyed the cave and ledge, only a couple yards away. It might as well have been miles. "How'd you get over there?"

"Will used a grapple." Lettie seemed proud of herself for knowing the correct term. She pointed, and Gina saw a rope tied to a metal pin in the rocky wall beside her. The other end was fastened near the cave entrance. "You just have to detach from your rope and slide over on that one. Easy!"

Right. Like that was going to happen. Ever.

"Here." Will jumped up on the rope and darted across it on hands and feet like a monkey. "I'll help you get your harness on this rope, then you can release the other rope."

Gina's fingers tightened on her rope.

"Maybe I should go first," Doctor Richards offered.

Even watching the others climb over her to reach the rope and safely slide across didn't do a thing for Gina's nerves. She berated herself the whole time, trying to kick her fears into submission, but nothing would coax her fingers to loosen.

Dieter was the last, aside from her. "I can help," he offered. "Lean on me, and I'll hold you up while he switches your harness over."

Her head shook no before she could consciously decide if she approved his offer or not.

"No problem," Will said. "I've helped shy climbers before. I know just the thing."

He probably had some magic trick up his sleeve. Some special words to say that would make her hands stop being stupid and uncooperative. Or something. She felt her shoulders relax, though her hands still wouldn't. He'd fix things, and it'd be okay.

Dieter paused, but let Will help him transfer his harness, then slid down the rope to the other side.

"Come on, Gina, it's easy," Lettie coaxed.

Great. Now she felt even more like an idiot.

"No problem," Will repeated, his tone cheerful. "Hang onto this real quick."

She managed to pry one hand loose to hold the jutting rock he pointed her to.

He grabbed a loop from her harness and connected it to something on the zip line. "Hey, big guy! You ready?"

She glanced back. Savion stood next to the other end of the rope, looking as stoic as ever. What were they planning? She hated to admit it, but Savion's presence didn't do much to help her feel better.

"Okay, here we go." Will pulled out a knife and reached for her rope a short distance above her hands. "You might want to hold your harness now."

Her eyes widened. "Wait! No, don't—"

He grinned and cut her rope.

Gina screamed. Everything blurred as she dropped, free-falling for a couple feet, then flew through the air. Her body slammed into something solid.

"See? Easy!" Lettie gushed.

Gina managed to crack one eye, unsure when she'd closed them this time. Savion set her upright. Her feet found solid rock, and he walked away.

Heat flooded her face. "I'm sorry. I mean, I was… I tried, but…"

"No problem," Will said, already back at her side. He helped her disconnect her harness. "You're not the first shy climber I've worked with."

She doubted he had many repeat customers with that sort of approach. But she kept the thought to herself; she might have to rely on his help again before this was over. With any hope, though, this was the last cliff edge they'd have to deal with before finding the ruby.

"We will continue now," Savion said, waiting at the cave entrance.

"Let's take a moment to check the book." Dieter held his hand out to Gina. "Just to see what we should watch for when we go in."

Gina dug into her bag and handed the journal over with shaking hands. She was grateful for his surreptitious way of giving her an extra minute to recover.

Will tucked the harness back in his bag and leaned closer to Gina. "You're not the first one who needed a little help getting started. It's a real rush, isn't it? I knew you'd love it."

She stared at him, speechless. Apparently he'd gotten the impression that her screams were based on thrill, like a kid on a roller coaster. She wasn't entirely sure how to explain to him that it was quite the opposite.

"The warnings seem fairly standard for a Mevoyan sacred place." Dieter flipped a couple more pages, skimming. "The gem is sacred, only the pure of heart may take it in hand, those who would seek to use it must cleanse themselves and prove their devotion by passing the trials, and so on."

"Trials?" Lettie asked.

"Getting past the traps." Gina smoothed her clothes, feeling better and more in control. Especially with her feet on solid ground.

"Traps?" the wiry worker asked. He looked worried.

Lich laughed. "Don't be scared, Shrimpy." She flexed her bicep in a mockingly masculine display. "I'll keep ya safe."

Most of the other workers joined her laughter.

Shrimpy glared at her. "I'm not scared." His eyes flicked toward Dieter. "I just think we should know what kind of traps we should be watching for."

"Watch for pressure plates—sections of the floor that look a bit higher than the rest of the floor, for instance. There may be levers on the walls, but avoid touching any of those unless we say it's safe." Dieter raised an eyebrow at Gina, inviting her to contribute.

She hesitated. Those were the main trap mechanisms found in other Mevoyan sites, and she wasn't sure there was much else she could mention. "That… that's kind of it. Just watch for those."

Burke eyed Dieter. "Good to know we at least have one brain leading us."

"Sure, Mr. Genius," Lich said. "Because you're contributing so much. Handing out water bottles and Band-Aids takes some real smarts."

Burke's eyes narrowed.

"Sheila," Owen barked, giving Lich the stink eye. "You're here to work, not jabber."

Gina would have edged back away from the whole mess if she wasn't standing only a couple feet from the ledge. Though the steep drop-off was almost looking preferable to all this bickering.

Dieter handed the journal back to her. "Let's get moving."

The others quieted down, but Gina didn't miss a few last death glares passing back and forth. She looked away from them, feeling the awkward tension like a tangible fog coating the group, and instead took in her surroundings. The cave entrance was only a little taller than human height, but wide enough for four or five people to comfortably walk side-by-side. The air remained still, marked only by a faint earthy scent and the distant drip of water. There were no signs any humans had been there before them.

"Doesn't look like an artifact site," Tad said, echoing her own thoughts.

"A wise move on the part of the Mevoyan people," Dieter replied. "What better way to hide a treasure than to leave the entrance untouched so casual explorers might not notice it?"

Tad shook his head, but they were already moving on.

The group fell quickly into a marching order with Will leading the way. Dieter and Gina walked just behind him to watch for signs of Mevoyan presence in ages past, especially in the form of traps. From the other sites that had already been discovered, Gina knew the traps could come at any moment. Some places had traps right at the entrance. Others didn't have any traps until quite a ways in. It was impossible to tell which this would be.

She felt like someone was watching over her shoulder and glanced back to find Savion behind her. An involuntary shiver slipped down her spine. She quickly turned her attention forward. He was watching her. Judging her. She hadn't really proven herself impressive or knowledgeable so far.

As light from the entrance faded behind them, they turned on the LED lanterns and headlamps Lettie had procured. Gina fumbled with her headlamp for a minute before giving up and opting to use the lantern instead, clipping it to her belt loop.

The new light sources flashed over something ahead that caught her eye. Uneven floor. "Hold up!"

Will stopped and looked back at her. "Did you forget something?"

She carefully angled her lantern to get a better view of the uneven patch, her heart thumping in her chest. A pressure plate for a trap? Fear warred with thrill. Traps meant danger, but they also meant they'd found the right place.

"What do you see?" Dieter asked, aiming his headlamp at the same area.

"I think there's a…" She moved around Will and stepped closer, trying to get a better view.

Fudgesicles. It wasn't a trap. Just an uneven spot in the floor. She turned back around to find a dozen lights shining in her face. Everyone was staring at her, waiting.

Her cheeks flamed. She fidgeted and searched for a way to gracefully salvage the moment. "I thought I saw something. Sorry. We can keep going."

She couldn't see Tad, but she could practically hear him rolling his eyes.

"That's okay," Will said, patting her shoulder as he passed her. "Good for you, being careful."

A few grumbles from the larger group suggested that not everyone shared his opinion. She exhaled and fell back in place behind Will, her cheeks still too warm. "Sorry," she mumbled to Dieter.

"Nothing to be sorry for."

They walked over the uneven patch with no problems and carried on. Gina set her jaw, determined not to make an idiot of herself again.

The cave gradually narrowed over the first half hour of walking, their progress slowed by the need to carefully navigate the uneven ground and occasional stalagmite or similar protrusions. Will chattered away the entire time, describing how certain formations would have come to be or how striations in the walls reminded him of other caves in other areas of the world.

"When people say 'it's a small world,' they usually don't really grasp how true that is," he jabbered on, walking backwards a few steps while easily side-stepping a jutting rock. "You could blindfold me and stick me in a cave, and when you take the blindfold off, I couldn't tell you if I was in Asia, Europe, Africa, or here. It's all the same on the inside." He grinned. "Stick that in your Disney movie."

Gina found the prattle annoying at first. She wanted to keep her focus on the path ahead, watching for potential traps. Besides, if she was right, she was among the first people to walk into this cave since the Spanish explorers found it centuries ago. She wanted to absorb the moment, to soak in the surroundings, to feel a proper sense of awe, and it was hard to do any of that with their guide trying to imitate a Chinese guy he'd spent three years spelunking with.

But as they passed their first hour of walking, the path grew narrower and more difficult, requiring them to walk single-file at times or even turn sideways and scoot through. Will quieted down during those passages. She felt awe for the first minute of silence, then the sense of awe quickly faded into a sense of oppression. The cave was too quiet. Too narrow. Too dark. Sweat tickled her forehead, and her chest began to ache from the tension. She began looking forward to his jabber sessions. They provided needed levity to the somber surroundings.

The second hour dragged by. As they scooted, crawled, climbed, and trudged on, Gina began wondering if she'd missed something. Dieter was right that a normal-looking cave entrance was the best disguise, but shouldn't they have seen something by now? Every bump in the floor set her heart into double-time, sure they'd finally found the first trap, but each time it was merely a natural part of the cave floor. She went back over the murals and writings in her mind but came to the same conclusion as before. The directions clearly said they were looking for a cave entrance in a downward direction from Pájaro Rojo. This had to be it.

Will slowed. "Whoa."

She blinked and looked up from the narrow spot she was squeezing through.

The tunnel opened up into a space over a story high, fifty feet wide, and a hundred feet long. The uneven, natural cave floor melted into a near-perfect grid of cobblestones that created a path through the middle of the space.

She gasped. A cobblestone path. Her mind raced so fast she could barely breathe straight. They'd found it. They'd found it!

# Chapter 4

Still frozen in awe, Gina drank in the scene. The cobbles were amazingly intact for their age, with only a few chips and breaks, though a few of the stones were missing entirely. Her eyes followed the path to a larger, grander tunnel ahead. Unlike the one she'd just left, the one ahead was clearly smoothed and widened by man-made tools. Gray-green columns stood sentinel on either side of the tunnel.

Her gaze continued upward, to the top of the columns. Her breath caught as her eyes fixed in place, lit up with the effervescent joy of discovery. Carved symbols decorated the wall above the tunnel. Five Mevoyan words that she knew all too well.

"The Temple of the Ruby of Ages," she whispered. Tears pressed at the corners of her eyes as her body buzzed with a new sort of energy, one that made her want to bounce on her toes like an excited schoolgirl.

A soft intake of breath behind her marked Dieter's entry into the space. He hovered behind her, soaking it in for a moment, then pulled her aside so the others could get through.

His touch broke the spell of awe holding her in place. She spun and grabbed his hands, barely able to contain herself. "This is it! We found it. We really found it!"

His grin nearly cracked his face. "We did indeed."

She impulsively threw her arms around him in a quick squeeze, then turned to Lettie as soon as her petite friend made it through. "We found it!"

Lettie squealed and all but jumped on her.

Savion took a bit longer to work his larger frame through the passage, but slowed at the sight. He moved to the other side of the path from them, never taking his eyes off the temple entrance.

Gina skittered closer, crouching to examine the stones, then dug out her camera. They were the first ones in this temple since the Spaniards marched through centuries ago. She had to record every moment, document every artifact they found. It almost made her squeal like Lettie. She'd scoured these reports from other scholars who'd discovered the other Mevoyan sites. Now she was the one doing the discovering.

A heavy foot clomped down on the cobblestones in front of her. "So this is it, huh?" Burke asked.

"No!" Gina jumped up and reached to push him back off the path.

He caught her arm and shoved it away. "What the heck is your problem?"

Dieter's firm hand clamped on the man's arm, pulling him back. "Don't walk on the path until we've had a chance to document it."

Burke yanked his arm free and glared. "It's just some stupid rocks. And we're gonna have to walk on them if we're gonna keep going."

"It's important to document everything," Lettie declared importantly. "If anything breaks or changes while we go through, we have to have a record of how it originally looked." She turned to Gina. "Right?"

"Right."

Burke rolled his eyes.

"Then this would be a good time to rest and eat something. And drink plenty of water," Dr. Richards instructed, setting her pack down near the side wall, a respectful distance from the cobblestone path.

The work crew seemed all too happy to take a break, though some dropped their loads a little closer to the path than Gina preferred. She did her best to angle the camera to keep the sweaty workers and modern packs out of the shots.

"You, too." The doctor's tone was almost scolding. "I can almost hear your stomach rumble from over here."

Gina hadn't noticed her stomach growling. She felt the urge to blush, but ignored it, still too caught up in her discovery. She did take a swig of water between photos and allowed Lettie to press a protein bar in her hands. It tasted slightly better than peanut butter smeared between layers of cardboard.

"This is it, huh?" Will stood a few feet behind her, munching on his own power bar. "You were right and that other guy was wrong."

A new feeling of delight swelled through Gina, one she was a bit less proud of. "Well, it was an easy error, since the wording—"

"Told you she's a genius," Lettie said, grinning. "These two are way better than that Kaufman guy."

"Congratulations," Will said to Gina. "This must be pretty huge for you."

"This is really it?" Tad asked around a mouthful of food. He gestured to the columns. "You actually found it?" He sounded much more surprised than Gina's ego preferred.

"Yes," Dieter said. "I believe we've already established that."

"So we might actually find this ruby. This great, big, giant ruby." Gina could practically see cartoon dollar signs floating in his eyes.

"That's the goal." Dieter took the camera from Gina and snapped a few photos closer to the tunnel entrance, careful not to step on the path in the process.

"How much did you say this thing was worth?"

Dieter looked up from the camera and frowned at him. "Don't be crass."

"I'm not. I'm just wondering, you know, out of curiosity."

Savion stood. "It is my people's greatest lost treasure." His face remained impassive, but his tone made his disdain for the conversation clear.

Tad faltered as if trying to find another way to word the same question, but he finally shut his mouth and sat down.

Gina and Dieter spent over an hour taking pictures, recording their observations, and examining every angle they could. Gina used the camera's zoom function to get a better view of the writing, of the depth of each letter, of the tool marks that formed them. She studied the columns with the hairline cracks hinting at their age and the cobblestones with their many colors suggesting that at least some had been imported through trade with far-off villages.

Lettie finally approached her. "Are we ready to get moving again?"

Gina glanced around; she'd practically forgotten that she and Dieter weren't the only ones in the room. Though many of the others had reacted with appropriate awe and curiosity on finding the space, almost all of them sat on the floor or leaned against the bare walls now, waiting with bored looks on their faces.

She cast a helpless look at Dieter. The thought of walking on these cobblestones, of risking damaging them further, sickened her. But it was the only way forward.

"We got everything we can. It's all on record," he said.

He was right. They might accidentally damage the stones by walking on them, but they had documented the untouched path. The scholarly world would understand, especially with what awaited them further in the caves.

The reminder of their ultimate goal lightened her internal struggle. Finding the ruby was the key part. She straightened but kept her camera in hand. "Okay."

"Can I…?" Lettie stood at the edge of the path, looking at Gina with eager eyes.

A voice inside Gina whispered that she was the one to figure out the correct translation, so she should have the honor of being the first one to step on the path. But she quickly silenced it with a mental scold. Without Lettie's money, they'd never have even made it to South America in the first place. "Go ahead."

Lettie delicately stepped onto the path. The stones didn't shift or crack, as Gina had feared they might. Apparently the construction was sturdier than she'd expected, despite its age.

Lettie grinned and took another step, then another. "I can't believe I'm really walking on—"

"Stop!" Savion shouted.

"Why?" Lettie asked, completing her next step. The stone her foot landed on sank a couple inches.

An overpowering sound of rock grinding against rock filled the space.

Lettie shrieked and jumped back. "It's caving in!"

Will frowned, looking far less concerned than Gina thought he should, and tilted his head toward the grinding sound. "That's not a cave-in. Not sure what it is."

A trap. Gina's gaze searched the tunnel, trying to find the source of the noise. Rocks falling? The way closing ahead? Or something else opening?

The rumbling sound ceased. No one moved for a few minutes, tense, waiting for something to come flying out at them.

Nothing happened.

"What was that?" Tad asked, sounding unimpressed.

"I'm not sure." Gina dug out her journal and leafed through it, but found nothing specific enough to clue her in. "There are supposed to be several traps along the way, but the writings didn't explain all the traps, probably because they were common to Mevoyan safeguards and would have been known to any Mevoyan trying to enter." She glanced at Savion. He'd spotted the trap first.

Dieter's gaze followed hers. He addressed Savion. "You knew the trap was there?"

Savion shook his head. "I only saw it before she stepped."

"How'd you know?" Lettie peered at the area at her feet. "They all look the same."

He looked away. "I recognized the pattern from stories of my people."

Gina squinted at the area. There was no pattern she could see. If he saw something that made that particular stone stand out, he must have superhuman sight.

"I'll take a peek and see if I can figure out what happened," Will said, starting forward.

"I will come," Savion said.

"Me, too," Dieter offered. He glanced back at Gina. "You should probably stay back with the others, just in case."

She nodded, feeling partly relieved. She glanced down the tunnel and chewed her hangnail. "Make sure nothing gets damaged."

"I'll do the best I can."

The three men walked forward, Will and Dieter studying the walls and ceiling while Savion's focus remained on the ground.

"There it is," Will said, stepping forward and turning to the wall a few yards into the tunnel. His upper half vanished into what must have been an opening. "Whoa."

"What?" Gina called.

Dieter craned his neck to see over Will, then waved her forward. "You can all come in. It's safe."

Gina hurried in, Lettie at her side. The others followed at a more casual pace.

Will stepped aside as the women reached him, revealing a large opening like a window in the intricately carved wall. Gina could see the portion of rock that had moved aside to create the opening, making the grinding noise. Gray, paper-like structures pocked with occasional holes filled the wide space on the other side of the window.

Will shone his light inside. "Looks almost like wasp nests, but not quite."

"It must have been some sort of stinging insect colony," Dieter said. "They trapped it behind this wall to be unleashed on intruders."

"So why aren't they here?" Lettie asked.

Dieter chuckled. "That was hundreds of years ago. The colony either died out or moved somewhere with more plentiful food sources."

"Oh."

"Well, that was a dud of a trap," Tad said. "Lame."

Gina barely noticed his comment. Her attention had turned to the walls of the tunnel behind them. "These are sacred patterns." She lifted her camera and recorded the carved lines decorating the walls in intricate designs. "Reserved for their most powerful and holy places."

"Are we, like, disturbing your ancestors or something?" Tad asked Savion.

"No." He looked over the wall with the polite curiosity of a museumgoer. "We do not practice the same beliefs as our ancestors."

"I guess we're safe to continue, then," Will said. He glanced down at the floor. "Maybe you should walk near the front, Savion. In case there are any more of those traps."

Savion nodded and walked to Will's side.

They fell back into their slightly modified marching order. Gina drank in the surroundings, snapping as many photos as she could. Will had quieted down, but she didn't mind this time. The silence now felt more like proper awe than oppression.

The sacred carvings in the walls were only occasionally interrupted with paintings, but the paintings only illustrated the ruby rather than providing any new information of what to expect ahead. She still paused to photograph each one, angling her lantern to get the best light.

The walls eventually faded back to natural rock, though some spots had obviously been altered with tools to maintain a relatively even width throughout the tunnel. Will and Savion kept their eyes open for signs of danger, and Gina and Dieter watched for hints of anything familiar from the writings, but time began to drag by as they continued through the winding, monotonous passage.

"We sure this is the right place?" Burke asked.

"Yeah," Tad said. "What he said. Shouldn't we be seeing more carvings and stuff if we're really getting closer? We must've missed something back there."

"This is normal for Mevoyan temples," Dieter explained. "They made their entrances elaborate, but the hallways are mostly undecorated. They believed firmly in sacredness in natural form and avoided shaping their environment when possible, especially in their holy places."

"That sounds dumb," Tad said. He jutted his chin toward Savion. "No offense or anything."

"No offense?" Lich snorted. "You're a moron. No offense or anything."

Other workers laughed and high-fived.

Gina adjusted her backpack and tried to ignore them. She leaned forward to see around Savion. It was definitely less awkward with him in front of her instead of behind, but she had a harder time seeing the path ahead around his bulk.

Will's headlamp beam flashed over something that caught her eye. "What's that?" she asked, hoping to find more writings, more clues to direct them.

Will turned his headlamp to better illuminate the upcoming area. The tunnel narrowed to a door-shaped space that spat them into a broad, round room with a domed ceiling. Savion had to duck at the entrance, but the ceiling quickly rose until it loomed high above even his head.

Gina gasped as she lifted her lantern. The opposite wall was so far away that her lantern's light couldn't reach it. The same cobblestones formed the floor, and she held back for a moment, afraid of more traps.

But Savion continued to the middle of the room without slowing his stride. "It is safe."

As the others filed in, the combined light chased the shadows back. The walls were formed of uniform, flat stones arranged in a grid much like the cobblestone floor, but reddish in tone instead of gray. At eye level, cream-toned stones formed a stripe around the room. Gina sucked in a breath as she saw exactly what she'd hoped for: writing. Mevoyan symbols filled the stripe in multiple distinct passages, each section of writing taking up several stones. A row of blank stones separated the passages from each other.

The overwhelming sense of awe returned as she took it all in. So much writing. And paintings. Painted illustrations decorated the walls above and below the stripe. The entire domed ceiling held a depiction of the sun stretching beams across the sky.

Her hands moved without much conscious thought, lifting the camera and snapping photos.

"Amazing," Dieter whispered.

"Where's the exit?" Tad asked.

The spell once again broken, Gina lowered the camera and looked around. She hadn't noticed that the room had no exit, only the opening they'd entered through.

"Great. We came all this way for some cave scribbles," Burke said.

"Sit down and give us some time to translate. There may be a hidden exit," Dieter said, sounding only mildly irritated.

"This might be the Room of Closure," Gina mused. "Which means there will be a way through to a Room of Safety."

The others were content to lounge and munch on snacks while Gina and Dieter worked their way around the room, her using the journal for reference while he copied their translations into the blank notebook. The space was occasionally lit up as Lettie carefully photographed everything, the writing and the paintings alike.

"Great trees through hearts," Gina mumbled, hovering her finger above the first few symbols.

"Strength. Great strength in hearts," Dieter corrected, writing it down. "This part is saying that whoever wishes to see the ruby will have to have courage."

"How's that supposed to help?" Tad called.

"Silence," Savion said, giving him a severe look. "Let them work."

To Gina's surprise, Tad obediently shut his mouth, though he didn't look happy about it.

She pointed to the part Dieter had translated about wishing to see the ruby. "That's an odd syntax, isn't it?"

He shrugged. "Their language, not ours."

They moved on to the next section. "Empty ocean of death."

"Pool. Empty pool of death." Dieter frowned. "Is that symbol what I think it is?"

She squinted at the one he pointed to, then nodded, surprised. "Siren."

"Siren?" Burke snorted. "I thought those were Greek mythology."

"It's the closest translation," Gina said. "The symbol refers to a female monster that lives underwater and lures people to their deaths. Kaufman likes to translate it as 'mermaid,' but Dieter and I think 'siren' is a better word for what the Mevoyan legends describe."

"So we're chasing legends now."

Dieter raised an eyebrow. "Because the Ruby of Ages is not considered a legend?"

That shut Burke up.

Tad spoke as if Burke had passed him a baton. "Sirens weren't water creatures, though. They were winged and lived on cliffs." His tone held the typical college student 'my class read about this topic once so now I'm an expert' tone.

"According to Greek writings, yes. But according to Roman writings, they were linked to the sea, as the daughters of Phorcys," Dieter said. At Tad's blank look, Dieter raised an eyebrow. "The primordial sea god? And Ovid's writings portray them as originally nymphs."

Tad made a face. "Whatever."

"So they believed there's a siren in a pool of death," Gina said, pulling Dieter's attention back to the translation. "Or some sort of creature drawn to blood. It… let's see… That word's 'home,' right?"

"Sort of. Nest?"

She nodded. "It nests beneath the pool of death."

"The ruby's pool?"

"Maybe." She walked over to the next section. "They must have put some animal in the pool to guard the ruby and called it a siren to scare off any searchers. Whatever it was, it's probably long gone by now, like the bugs from that first trap."

"A safe assumption." He studied the symbols. "This part looks familiar—pure in heart."

"Right." Most of the section repeated a passage from another Mevoyan cave-inscription about the ruby. "This part's new. 'Cleanse and purify heart and limb.'"

"Hand. Heart and hand." He wrote it down.

"And none may journey—leave—until the pool… Huh." She peered at the symbol. "Is that blood? It's a different symbol than the other one for blood."

"It conveys the appearance rather than the actual substance," Dieter explained. "None may leave until the pool looks like blood."

"Blood?" Lettie asked. "There has to be blood in the pool?"

Dieter waved a hand dismissively. "Again, it's more related to appearance than substance. It may be some sort of light trick, or an algae, or it might have just been written to scare off the unworthy. We'll know more when we get there."

They continued their way around the room from the section to the right of the door to the last section on the left of the door. The other passages mostly seemed to repeat the same information they'd already found in other caves and artifacts.

"This one's new," Gina said, studying the last one. "Room of trick…"

"Puzzle."

"A puzzle room." Her eyes lit up. "This room."

"Keep going," he urged.

"Puzzle room to solve—will be solved, I mean—only by true of spirit."

"A true Mevoyan person," Dieter translated.

She glanced at Savion and found him watching them. She blushed and quickly returned her eyes to the writing.

Dieter looked back at the large man, less bashful. "So? Any special insights for this one?"

Savion shook his head.

"Great," Tad muttered.

Lettie finished her task and eyed the walls. "So what's that mean? We're stuck?"

"We'll figure it out," Gina assured her.

"They move," Savion said, his eyes fixed on the rocks forming the walls.

"What?" Dieter asked.

"They move. If you press on the rocks, they will move, like the trap before."

"Pressure plates." Gina took a step back from the wall. "More traps?"

"Or the solution to the puzzle," Dieter said. "If we press the right rocks, we'll get through."

"So which ones are the right ones?" Lettie asked. "How are we supposed to tell?"

Gina tapped her finger on her chin, frowning at the walls and wishing a neon sign would appear to highlight the answer.

"We could just try and see what works," Lettie suggested. She walked over and reached for one of the stones.

"No!" Dieter barked out, stopping her. "Pressing the wrong ones could activate a trap."

Lettie turned, her eyes glistening with excitement once more. "You're saying we have to find the right ones or be caught in a trap."

Gina returned her attention to the walls, leaving Lettie to her visions of Indiana Jones. There had to be some sort of key, some way of knowing which stones were the right ones to press. Something only a true Mevoyan person would identify.

What made a person a true Mevoyan? She tapped her chin again. Not birth alone. Savion was a true Mevoyan, but he had no idea. This puzzle required more than just biological backgrounds. It needed knowledge.

Her eyes shifted back to the first translation. Knowledge of the culture. Of the writings.

"Huh." She walked back to the first section.

"What?" Dieter asked, following her.

"You know this part with the weird syntax?"

He nodded.

"It's a weird syntax for this sentence, but not…" She pulled out her journal and found a picture from one of the first caves discovered. "Not when it's used in this sentence here." She compared the symbols. "That part's word for word, actually."

Dieter looked from the picture to the writing on the wall. "And it's all fit on one stone."

He was right. The improperly worded part all fit onto one of the dozen stones making up that section of writing. Excitement swelled in Gina's chest as she hurried to the next section, comparing it to their translation. "Here. The syntax on this stone is wrong, too, but it matches…" She flipped through the journal again until she found another picture. "Here, from that cave near the ocean they found ten years ago." She looked up, eyes shining. "It's also word for word."

Lettie chewed her bottom lip. "So… It's wrong… because…"

"They believed only a true member of their people would know all of their writings and recognize these stones." Gina couldn't stop grinning as she looked around the room. Every section of writing had one stone with incorrect syntax or grammar. She'd dismissed it as her own error when they translated the sections, but now she understood. "These are the stones we have to press to pass through this room."

"You figured it out!" Lettie cheered.

"Great," Burke said. "Which one do you press first?"

Gina's smile faded. "Uh…"

Dieter slowly turned to scan the sections. "There's nothing specifying an order. They write from right to left as we do, so perhaps we should just follow the sections around the room, starting at the entrance."

"You think that'll do it?" Will asked.

Gina racked her brain but couldn't come up with any better solution. "I think so. It might be that order doesn't matter, as long as we press all of the correct stones."

Lettie peered at the section on the right of the entry. "Could I do it?"

"Sure." Gina pointed to the correct stone.

Lettie took a deep breath and pushed.

The stone sank an inch into the wall. Rumbles echoed from behind the wall.

Gina took a step back, holding her breath. Had they been wrong?

The rumbles fell silent.

Everyone looked around, watching for something to happen, but nothing did.

"What did it do?" Tad finally asked. "Was it a dud like that other one?"

"I don't think so," Dieter said. "It's like a multi-part lock. The rumbling we heard was the first part of the lock opening."

Tad gave him a blank stare again.

"Here," Gina directed Lettie to the stone in the next section. "We won't know until we finish."

Lettie pushed. Again, the stone sank an inch. Again, rumbles, longer this time. Again, nothing happened.

"We're unlocking the door, aren't we?" Lettie's eyes once again glowed with visions of fictional archeologists.

"I think so." Gina pointed to the next one.

Lettie pushed. The rumbling started up, louder this time. And longer.

Gina looked around, a knot developing at the bottom of her stomach. Had she been wrong?

Savion looked up with a frown.

The dome trembled. Cracked. A massive section of rock broke free and fell in.

Gina screamed as Dieter pulled her and Lettie back from the walls. Tad barely jumped away from the entry in time to avoid being crushed.

The rock came to rest in the entrance, completely blocking the way out.

# Chapter 5

Gina cringed, ready to drop into a ball and cover her head if the rest of the dome collapsed in on them, but the rumbling ceased. Nothing else fell.

As the adrenaline faded, sadness rushed in. "The painting… we ruined it!" A massive dark spot marred the upper dome. It'd been almost pristine before they came. She was destroying the very artifacts she'd come to study.

"Great. I almost get squashed, and she's worried about arts and crafts," Tad grumbled.

Lettie patted Gina's shoulder. "I got all the pictures. We still have those."

Will looked around the sealed room. "Now what?"

"Obviously they got it wrong," Burke said. "Quit pushing those things before you bring the whole cave down on our heads."

"Solving the puzzle is the only way out of this room," Dieter said.

"Or to kill us all," Tad muttered.

"There's another way out." Burke pointed to the fallen rock. "Grunts, get that thing out of the way. We'll go back the way we came."

"No!" Lettie shook her head vehemently. "We didn't find the ruby. We can't leave without what we came for."

"We can't leave if we're all buried in a cave-in, either."

Dieter studied the walls once more. "We have two options. Move the rock and go back the way we came, or solve the puzzle and continue forward. Perhaps we should have Owen's team work on moving the rock. Anyone who wishes to leave may do so. But I, for one, believe this can be solved. We can move forward."

"Right." Gina gave him a smile. She knew he'd stick with it.

"I will help move the rock," Savion said.

She glanced at him, feeling a pang of disappointment. He was giving up?

"See?" Burke jabbed a thumb in Savion's direction. "Even the Mevoyan guy sees this is pointless."

"You misunderstand." Savion walked around the rock, studying it. "I will help. I will not leave."

Gina relaxed. He hadn't lost faith in them.

"Come on, grunts," Owen ordered, stuffing a food wrapper in his bag and standing. He stretched and popped a few joints. "Let's get this rock out of the way for the wimps who want to bail."

Several of the crew members laughed as they joined him. Tad and Burke both scowled.

Doctor Richards gave Owen a severe look. "If these men want to leave, that's their choice. There's no need to shame them for it."

Gina turned to Dieter, feeling significantly better. Most of the team was dedicated to the task. As for Tad and Burke, she couldn't say she'd miss them if they left. "What's our next move?"

"Either we have the order incorrect," Dieter mused, still studying the walls, "or this is a natural part of the unlocking process."

Will quirked an eyebrow toward the dark hole in curve of the dome. "You think that might be the exit?" Before anyone could answer, he jumped on the wall, avoiding the pressure stones, and scurried up to shine a light in the hole. "Nope. Dead end."

Dieter cleared his throat. "I only meant that it's not unheard of for a Mevoyan sacred place to be sealed before entrance is permitted."

Writings and images flashed through Gina's mind. "Of course! The writings talked about sacred places being kept separate from the outside through closure. I guess I always thought that was metaphorical, or that it was a moveable door of some sort."

"So we might have it right?" Lettie asked, hope returning.

"There's only one way to find out." Dieter pointed to the next section of writing.

"Hey, shouldn't we move this rock first?" Tad asked.

Owen fastened another rope to the pulley system his crew and Savion worked on. "Go ahead. We'll have this out of the way in a flash."

Lettie smiled and pushed the next stone.

Rumbling came from the hole. Followed by a rush of water.

Lettie shrieked and darted out from under the torrent, wet hair plastered to her face. The others yelled in surprise and scrambled back, but the water quickly pooled on the floor.

"Move the rock! Now!" Dieter shouted.

Gina backed to the middle of the room, staring in horror. The rock wasn't a perfect seal against the exit, but the trickle escaping its edges was no match for the gush of water thundering into the room. Water filled the space, fast. Too fast.

Owen shouted orders. Workers scrambling around to finish the last connections. Savion and several of the crew heaved ropes. The fibers creaked and groaned as the ropes strained against the obstacle. The rock budged an inch, then a rope snapped. The attached pulley went flying into the wall.

Will scrambled a few feet up the wall, prodding at the curve of the dome. "I can't find the other exit!"

The excitement of adventuring had vanished from Lettie's face, replaced by terror. "We're going to die!"

Panicked screams and cries filled the space, echoing in a frantic cacophony. Owen's crew, Savion, Tad, and Burke all struggled with the rock, but couldn't coax it to budge again.

Gina remained frozen in place, unable to think straight. She'd been wrong. And now they were all going to die.

Dieter's hands gripped her shoulders. He got in her face. "Think, Gina. We have the order wrong. What would the Mevoyan people have used to order the keys?"

Paintings, carvings, murals all flipped through her mind with no logical order or flow. "I don't know!"

"Yes, you do. You can do this. Give me ideas. What would a true Mevoyan person know that others wouldn't?"

The syntax. The grammar. They'd already gotten that part.

Water splashed at her knees. Swaying headlamps and lanterns cast bizarre, ethereal reflections of light off the rising surface. She shuddered.

"Focus."

She exhaled. Focused. Whoever designed this cave expected that anyone entering would know of the other writings. The other caves and murals.

Her eyes widened. "The other caves."

"Yes?" he prompted.

"They've been dated. They weren't all carved at the same time. They were written in a certain order."

Understanding dawned behind his own eyes. He spun, looking at the sections, and strode toward one near the door. "The Levick cave was first."

She caught his arm. "No, that was the first one discovered. But it's not the oldest." She looked around frantically until she spotted what she was looking for. She sloshed through the water to one of the sections in the middle. "This comes from the oldest writings on record."

Her own words sent a chill through her. What if there was another cave that hadn't been found yet? They could get the wrong order and not even know it.

"What are you two doing?" Burke shouted. "You're wasting time. Come help us already!"

The water was already mid-thigh. They'd be swimming before long. Maybe Burke was right.

Dieter struggled against the water to the rock and threw his shoulder into the work. "I'll help them. You solve the puzzle."

She clenched her teeth. Even with all the men pushing against it, the rock hadn't budged. She might be their only chance of making it out alive.

She pressed the stone.

It sank in. Something rumbled. Nothing changed.

She turned around, frantically calculating numbers and facts. There, writing from the second-oldest cave. She struggled through the waist-deep water and pressed the next stone.

It grew harder and harder to move through the water as she fought her way back and forth across the room, pressing the stones in the new order. By the fifth one, she had to duck her head underwater to find the right stone.

"Gina!" Lettie wailed as she surfaced. "Get us out of here!"

She didn't answer, keeping her focus on the task at hand. She swam to the next one.

Burke surfaced, sputtering. "It won't move!"

Gina ducked underwater again. Pushed the next stone. Three more to go.

Shouts and yells echoed all the more in the smaller space between the rising waters and the dome's top. Will fought his way toward the gushing hole. "I'll try to see if we can swim up it!" But even he wasn't making it very far, the powerful water forcing him back.

Gina dove to the next section. Two more to go.

Dieter appeared beside her on the surface. "Where?"

She struggled to keep her head above the churning water. "That one." She pointed to the first section by the door. "Then I'll push the last one over here." It wasn't far. She could reach it fast and be ready by the time he pushed the one by the door.

Dieter vanished beneath the water.

Only a foot remained between the water and the dome. The surface roiled as people thrashed, fighting to stay in the vanishing air pocket.

Gina held her breath and dove once more. Found the correct stone. Turned to see if Dieter had pressed his.

The water remained inky black down here. The LED lights in her lantern only pierced an arm's length into the darkness. It hadn't occurred to her that she wouldn't be able to see him.

She clawed to surface. Inches remained. "Dieter, did you get it?"

No answer.

"Dieter!"

The water rose. She sucked in one last breath and swam back down to the last stone. They were out of time. Dieter had better have pressed the stone by the door by now, or they were all dead.

She closed her eyes and pushed the stone.

A rumble tore through the water, the sound only slightly dimmed and distorted by the liquid surrounding her. The water rushed toward the exit. Gina scrambled back up to find a foot-high gap at the surface. Two feet. The water level was dropping.

"You did it," Lettie gasped, treading water.

Relieved cheers filled the widening space.

Gina turned, searching. "Dieter?"

"Here." He swam to her side, looking exhausted. "I tried to signal you, but—"

"The water was too dark, I know." She smiled. "I knew you'd gotten it."

His own lips tipped upward, his dark hair sticking to his forehead.

As the water finally deposited their feet back on the floor, Gina saw what had happened. The rock now sat a couple feet lower than before, creating an exit for the water. The flow from above had ceased, as well.

"Great. Just about got us all killed," Tad muttered, wringing futilely at his shirt. He let out an exclamation and dug into his pack, emerging with his tablet computer. "It's ruined! You ruined it!"

Will stared at him like he was an idiot. "You brought something like that on a cave expedition?"

Tad scowled and jabbed at Will's GPS. "You brought your stuff."

"It's designed for this sort of thing." Will tapped the device. "Waterproof."

Tad continued scowling but said nothing else.

Burke studied the gap at the exit. "Most of us should be able to fit through this. We can send help."

Gina looked around. No new entrance had opened. But they'd pressed the rocks in the right order, hadn't they? The vanishing water was proof of that.

"Hold on." Dieter stood with head tilted slightly, as if listening. He slowly scanned the opposite wall. "Just wait."

She looked where he looked, trying to figure out what he seemed to suspect. What did they know? The Room of Closure would be followed by a Room of Safety. Somewhere safe.

An idea started to take hold. It wouldn't be safe if it was full of water.

"Wait? For what?" Burke demanded.

Neither Dieter nor Gina answered.

"Well?" Burke pushed.

Savion spoke. "Wait."

The water lowered to a puddle around their ankles, then a faint trickle vanishing through the remaining cracks at the entry.

A new rumbling sound shook the walls.

"Not again!" Lettie gasped.

"It's okay," Gina said, still staring at the opposite wall. Was it just her imagination, or were some of the cracks between the stones widening?

It wasn't her imagination. The cracks widened further until the shape of a door formed. The room trembled as the door slowly descended into the ground, leaving behind an opening. The exit.

Lettie whooped.

"It seems you found the way through," Doctor Richards said, trying to get her hair back into some semblance of order. "But I recommend we take a moment here to rest and recover."

Dieter approached the exit, shining his light through it. "We've got the perfect place for that here."

Gina hurried to join him. "The Room of Safety."

The room on the other side of the doorway was twice the size of the one they stood in, though arranged in a rectangular shape rather than a dome. Many stone slabs lined the room, cracked and crumbling leathers spread over them. Beds. Dust-covered jars filled nooks set into the stone walls as well as covering a sort of table at the far end. A circle of stones almost waist high and covered with a heavy slab marked the middle of the room. The space was large enough to allow for plenty of sitting and moving space between the circle in the middle and the beds at the edges. On the other side of the room, a dark tunnel led away from the room deeper into the cave system.

Tad leaned over Gina's shoulder and glared. "Probably another trap."

"Not this one." Gina stepped into the room, awed by her surroundings. "It's a Room of Safety." She realized more explanation was needed for those unfamiliar with ancient Mevoyan culture. Namely, everyone except her and Dieter. "The Mevoyan people created special caves throughout their territory, places where warriors could safely rest and recover as needed. They're usually secured by traps, like this one was, but once you're inside the room, you're safe."

Lettie followed her in and poked at one of the leathers. It crumbled under her finger, and she jumped back. "I didn't do anything!"

"It's very old." Gina was aware her tone was like she was talking to a child, and she quickly tried to modify it. "I mean, it's fragile. Um, why don't you help everyone collect the gear while I check this stuff out?"

"I can take pictures."

The camera. Gina's stomach plummeted briefly before she remembered the camera was supposed to be waterproof. "Did the camera come through okay?" They hadn't exactly tested it before leaving. If they'd lost all those pictures…

Lettie lifted the camera and clicked a picture of Gina. "Perfect working order." She beamed.

Gina exhaled in relief. She let her friend control the camera once more while she examined the artifacts in the room. Dieter wandered to the end of the room and studied the jars.

While the three of them worked, Will directed the rest of the group to load the gear into the large, open space in the middle of the room. Once the gear was safely in, the others began wringing out their clothes and surveying the damage caused by the water.

Will approached Gina and tapped her shoulder, leaning in like a child who never learned the concept of personal space. "I know you wanted to keep going, but we have to turn back."

Dieter approached, frowning. "What are you talking about?"

The younger man glanced back over his shoulder at the others, then craned his neck even closer. "Everyone's soaking wet. We'll become hypothermic before long down here unless we can find a way to get dry. We have to go back up, dry out, and try again. Probably tomorrow."

Gina cringed. Kaufman would likely figure out by then that he'd gotten it wrong. And she wasn't convinced she could trust him to keep his promise not to enter their cave.

Dieter looked equally displeased. "We can't go back now."

"We can't stay here." Will shrugged. "Sorry."

Gina glanced over at the others. Several shivered hard enough for their trembling to be visible, even from across the room. Now that she was distracted from the euphoria of discovery, she had to confess that her own legs shook. The cold of the room seemed to seep through her whole body. As much as she hated to admit it, Will was right. They'd get sick or even die if they didn't get dry.

Her eyes fell on the stone circle in the middle of the room. Images and writings clicked into place. She smiled. "What if we could start a fire down here and dry off?"

Will raised an eyebrow. "Even if we had anything dry to burn, we'd be filling the room with smoke. We have to go up to surface."

Dieter saw her focus and nodded. Without a word, he strode to the circle and tugged at the slab. It barely scraped an inch. "Savion?"

The larger man joined him, and the two of them lifted the slab aside. Gina stepped closer to see, hoping she'd been right.

She had. Dark liquid reflected in the light from Dieter's headlamp.

"What's that?" Lettie asked, snapping a couple more pictures.

"Oil." Dieter gestured around the room. "This space was designed for warriors to safely rest, remember. They would've needed a fire to keep warm and cook over, too."

"And the smoke?" Will asked.

"Yeah, dying of smoke inhalation sounds a lot better than dying of hypothermia," Burke added unnecessarily.

Gina craned her neck. The ceiling vanished into darkness high above them, but a few pinpricks of light dented the inky blackness. "It's vented. We can light the oil."

Lettie's face brightened once more. "We're going to light ancient oil that was put here thousands of years ago. It's like something out of a movie!"

Will pulled out a waterproof match container and lit the oil. It immediately flared to life, orange flames dancing over the surface.

"Get close," Doctor Richards commanded. "No one leaves this room until everyone is dry and warm."

Most of the men stripped off their upper layers, laying the clothes on the rocks around the blazing oil. Gina's face flamed when a few even pulled off their pants and spread those out, as well.

Lich elbowed her way closer to the fire and tossed her own shirt and pants onto the rocks. Whoops rose from the men, but she didn't seem slightly embarrassed to stand with the men in just her undergarments. Instead, the muscled woman grinned broadly. "Enjoy it while it lasts. I know every one of you boys, and this is the closest any of you are *ever* going to get."

A few of the other female workers joined her, seemingly unperturbed by the continued leers and catcalls from the men.

Gina did her best to stand close to the fire while keeping her eyes on the ceiling above.

Burke pushed in next to her. She glanced down to adjust her footing and quickly jerked her attention back up when she caught a glimpse of boxers.

"Sorry," he said in a tone which made it clear he wasn't remotely sorry. "Didn't mean to make you blush."

Dieter's firm hand put a more comfortable distance between Burke and Gina. He stepped into the space, thankfully still wearing pants.

The oil burned hot and bright, and soon Gina felt the chill melting away. The clothes near the fire steamed as they warmed and dried. Workers continued jabbering and joking, some of the men getting into testosterone matches over their respective muscle sizes or ability to impress the girls. Gina was able to keep most of it to a background buzz around her, still working to ignore the excess of skin surrounding her, until a voice called in her direction.

"So what's your deal?" Petty asked. It took Gina a moment to realize he was talking to Dieter. "Couldn't keep up with the other boys, so you turned egghead?"

Owen's eyes narrowed, and his tone held a warning. "Petty…"

Dieter lifted a hand to brush away Owen's concern. "I've always had an interest in history. The Mevoyan culture fascinated me from the start. Their approach to life was unique among the tribes in this region. While other peoples considered warriors to be the highest tier of society, the Mevoyan people placed a higher emphasis on spirituality and artistry. While their warriors were certainly honored and valued, the artisans—"

"Snore." Petty rolled his eyes. "I get it. Your daddy couldn't get you to play football, so you're trying to find a big gem to prove you've still got something in your pants."

Owen opened his mouth again, but Lich beat him to it with a snort. "Right. Because every little boy dreams of growing up to be a two-bit grunt like you."

"Whatever. At least I know I've got it where it counts. Not like—"

"Shut it," Jake said, planting himself in front of Petty. The larger man towered over him, but Jake didn't flinch.

"That's enough," Owen said, his voice a bit darker and louder than before.

Petty glared his way, then shrugged and backed off.

Gina glanced at Dieter. The muscles around his mouth were tight. "Ignore him," she said quietly, feeling stung on her friend's behalf. "He's being stupid. Everyone knows—"

"It's fine," Dieter said, his tone strained.

She shut her mouth.

After a moment, he exhaled. "I apologize. That was rude."

"No, I shouldn't have pushed."

He waved a hand dismissively again. "I shouldn't have let him get to me, and I shouldn't have snapped at you."

She shifted her gaze back to the ceiling. How had Petty's words gotten to Dieter? He'd always been the most confident, secure man she'd ever known. He hardly seemed the type to be bothered by such immature taunts. "You know, everyone here admires you. The work you do takes real smarts and commitment. And—"

He laughed, sounding amused, but quickly caught himself. "Sorry. No, that's not what the problem was."

Though part of her told her it was rude to pry into someone else's business, the rest of her brain had found a puzzle and latched onto it like a kid on cotton candy. "Then it was... what he said about finding the ruby? You don't think you have to prove something by finding it, do you?"

His eyes took a distant look. He didn't answer.

"Sorry. It's not my business."

"My father... let's just say he and I had issues."

She glanced at him. She hadn't remembered hearing much about his family. They'd always talked about their studies, but rarely their personal lives. Some friend she was. "You don't have to talk about it if you don't want to."

He shook his head. "But this isn't about his approval. I'm not even seeking the ruby for myself, really."

"It's for the remaining Mevoyan people." Like her. Sure, it'd be nice to see her name in the books. And to see the look on Kaufman's face when he realized how thoroughly he'd been bested. But her biggest hope was to see the general public become aware of this lost culture, to see the few remnants honored as they should be.

He cast a sideways smile at her. "For the people."

It took an hour before the items were dry enough to be collected. Owen directed the men to tend to the gear, giving Gina, Lettie, and the other clothed women a little privacy near the fire.

By the time Gina was dry enough to venture away from the flames, her clothes stiff and her skin feeling tight from the heat's quick work, the others had already started laying out items near the fire to dry. Sleeping bags covered almost every square inch of floor.

Gina's heart sank in sudden fear. Her pack. The journals. She quickly dug in to find the items in the bag mostly dry. Of course. Lettie had made sure to get top-of-the-line gear. The packs must be water-resistant. Gina dug out the two books and found only minor water damage around the edges. The sleeping bag, which attached to the outside of the pack, had gotten the worst of it. She unrolled it and shook it a few times, trying to get it to unfold completely and lie flat on the rock floor.

Will appeared at the other end and smoothed out the stubborn part. "There. It'll be dry in no time." He glanced at her open pack. "Were your books okay? These packs should be pretty solid, even with a dunking. They didn't get washed out, did they?"

She shook her head. "They're fine."

"Good. I know how important they are to you." He cleared his throat. "I mean, to us. Because that's what's guiding us." He glanced away, looking slightly embarrassed.

"Thanks," Gina said, accepting his quick cover with only a faint blush of her own.

"So, I checked out the tunnel. We've got a cave-in ahead," he reported. "We'll have to see if we can safely clear it before we can move on."

"A cave-in?" It was like the whole cave conspired to prevent them from reaching the gem. Though, when she thought about it, she realized that was sort of the point.

"I've dealt with these before. It doesn't look bad. I'm sure we'll be able to get it clear, as long as we're careful," Will reassured her. "I'll need a lot of light in there so I can make sure nothing else will come falling down on us while we're clearing, then I'll need some extra hands."

"You heard him," Owen barked. The work crew, most of which had been resting, jumped to their feet and headed into the tunnel.

"I'll see what I can do to help," Dieter said, following them. Savion joined him without a word.

Gina looked around, unsure of anything she could do to help, and finally decided to inventory the room. Lettie followed her around, examining everything while being careful not to touch.

The walls were mainly bare. A few paintings here and there marked the room's safety and connection to the Ruby of Ages, but there was nothing new or unique on the walls. After Gina ensured each painting had been properly recorded, she moved on to the jars. It didn't look like Dieter had opened any, but disturbances in the dust showed where he'd picked up a couple of them.

"You already got pictures of all of these?" she asked Lettie.

"Yup. Every one." Lettie lifted the camera and snapped a couple more shots anyway.

Gina lifted one of the jars Dieter had already disturbed and tested its weight in her hand. It felt heavier than it should be, even with the sandstone it was formed from. Full.

She inspected it carefully before she finally chanced the lid.

"Are you supposed to do that?" Lettie whispered.

"It's fine." Gina lifted the lid and studied the thick, amber-tinged substance inside.

"What is it?" Lettie hovered at her shoulder.

Gina sniffed it. "Honey."

"Honey?"

"Food to sustain the warrior." She smiled and set it down, then picked up the other jar. Its weight felt slightly different. Lighter, though just as full. She opened it and sniffed the inky sludge inside.

"Ew." Lettie wrinkled her nose.

"Medicine." Gina cupped the jar in her hands, overwhelmed again by awe. "This is what they used to treat their wounds." She'd read about it, but never seen any physical samples herself. And certainly none so old or authentic as this. And now she stood in a Mevoyan place of safety, surrounded by the honey and salves they'd stored for the care of their fighting men. Incredible.

Footsteps echoing through the tunnel and dancing lights announced the return of the workers. Gina stared. It hadn't been enough time to clear a cave-in, had it?

Will and Dieter walked straight to her. "We got it partially cleared," Will reported, "but we're going to have to go a bit slower for the next part. It's a good stopping point."

"Stopping?"

Dieter patted her shoulder. "It's almost ten. We've been at this all day now. We'll get some rest and start fresh in the morning."

"Ten?" She blinked, surprised. It was later than she'd thought. It was harder to gauge the passage of time so far underground. It occurred to her that it probably took quite a bit of time to translate all the text in the previous room; she just hadn't noticed how long it took since she was so excited to discover it.

Doctor Richards approached. "Anyone experiencing headaches?" When they shook their heads, she proceeded to rattle of a drug-commercial-worthy list of symptoms, eyebrow raised in wait for someone to confess to any of the named ailments. They all shook their heads again.

"Good." She looked satisfied. "Eat some dinner, then sleep as close to the fire as possible. Stay warm. If you develop any of the symptoms I named, let me know immediately."

"Will do," Gina promised. The doctor moved on, and Gina overheard her asking the same questions of the next group of people.

"Doctor's orders," Dieter said, pushing a freeze-dried ration pack into Gina's hands.

She rolled her eyes. Her traitorous stomach growled at the same time. She sighed and ate, then climbed into her sleeping bag. They'd rest, then start again in the morning. With any hope, they'd have the ruby in hand before the day's end.

With any hope.

# Chapter 6

Gina woke to an unforgiving crick in her neck and protesting muscles in her legs. She winced as she stretched all of the above, moving slowly to cater to the complaints. She'd never considered herself unhealthy or unfit, but yesterday's hike had far surpassed any of her former exercise regimens.

Will bounced around the cave as if he'd slept on a feather bed and downed a triple-espresso. "All right, we just have a bit more to go before the way's clear. Let's get moving!"

A few groans rose from the work crew, making Gina feel better.

Tad made more noise than all of them combined. "I think I slept on a rock!"

"We all slept on rock." Dieter's face remained expressionless, but Gina saw the laugh in his eyes.

Tad glared. "You know what I mean."

Owen wandered closer, peering into the shadows between the bed slabs where the light from the still-blazing oil fire didn't reach. "Have you guys seen Mick or Benito?"

If she had, she wouldn't know their names. "Um…"

"None of your crew came over this way," Dieter said. "They all kept pretty close together over on that side. Is something wrong?"

"No one's seen them this morning. Their gear is still here, but they're gone."

"They were smart," Tad grunted, still untangling his legs from his sleeping bag. "Snuck their way back to the exit and took off before they get killed by another screw-up like yesterday."

Gina blinked, first taken aback at the implied accusation, then surprised at the assumption, but it was possible. The exit from the domed room wasn't entirely blocked anymore. They could have squeezed through the space and left. But why leave their packs?

Owen looked displeased. "Without talking to me? I doubt it. And why would they have left their packs?"

Tad shrugged.

Dieter glanced back at the rest of the crew, then returned his focus to Owen. "I wasn't going to say anything, but I did hear some of your men talking about leaving while we worked on the cave-in yesterday. I know we were all shaken up by the incident yesterday, and I believed they were merely blowing steam, so I ignored it. Perhaps your two men took it a bit more seriously than I judged it to be. As for the packs, I'm not certain why they would have left them."

Owen's displeasure deepened, but he finally nodded. "I guess. They must've left the packs for us to have the extra supplies and just carried what they needed to get back out. Wish they'd come to me first, though." He turned and walked back to the rest of his crew, barking orders as he went.

After breakfast, Gina helped Lettie, Doctor Richards, and a few others help gather the gear back into packs while everyone else helped clear the last of the rocks blocking the path ahead. Tad and Burke both stayed behind on the pretense of helping pack the gear but mostly just griped and grumbled back and forth. It seemed to Gina that the two men were happiest when they had something to complain about.

It wasn't long before the others returned. Savion and Dieter lifted the slab back over the fire pit, smothering the oil fire. If they ran into any trouble ahead and needed a heat source again, they'd be able to reignite it without too much difficulty. That brought Gina some feeling of relief. If she messed up another translation, at least they had a safe place to get warm and dry.

They set out down the tunnel. The walls were once again natural rock only occasionally shaped by tools, but the floor remained the same cobblestone path. No paintings or writings decorated the walls. Gina kept her eyes ahead, peering around Savion to try to see as far ahead as possible.

The remnants of the cave-in still filled most of the tunnel, piled against the sides and littering the floor with a person-sized gap near the top. A gaping, dark hole above marked where the ceiling had collapsed. She wasn't sure if it had been a trap the Spaniards had set off or if it had just been the wear of passing centuries deteriorating the tunnel's integrity. A shiver slipped through her at the thought. They'd have to be extra careful, not just on the watch for traps but also for areas weakened by time.

Dieter gave her a hand climbing over the last of the loose rocks. A couple shifted under her feet, but the pile remained stable enough for everyone to cross safely. Her muscles whined at the unsteady climb. She told them to shut up. She didn't want the others to think she couldn't handle the trek or keep up.

The tunnel remained clear from there, staying mostly uniform in width and gradually descending. Time began to melt around Gina. The unchanging scenery made it that much harder to tell how many hours they'd been walking. Two? Three? Or was it only one, but just felt longer because of her aching legs and the lack of discoveries to keep her mind engaged?

She sighed.

"All right, experts," Will said, drawing her attention forward again. "Which way?"

The tunnel broadened in a triangular shape ahead, splitting off into three different tunnels. Gina checked the floor in hopes of an easy solution. All three paths were paved with the cobblestones. No paintings or symbols marked the walls, so all the tunnels looked just like the one they'd been walking through. They'd have to use other means to figure out which path to take.

She dug out her journal and flipped through the pages.

Dieter wandered closer and peered down each tunnel, his headlamp illuminating several yards down the lengths. "Do you think this might be the branching?"

"Probably."

"Branching?" Tad folded his arms. "That doesn't even make sense."

"It's the way the Mevoyan people described a sort of labyrinth in the rock," Gina said, flipping to the relevant images. "The writings include directions for how to navigate it."

"Right. Because following what's written worked so well last time."

She ignored him and found the beginning of the directions. "Okay, this one says to go eastward."

Will consulted the GPS. "None of these tunnels go east."

"It means right," Dieter explained. "The Mevoyan use of cardinal directions tends to be fluid and relative to the person's position." He gestured to the tunnel on the right.

Will stepped to the tunnel and shone his light along the walls, studying it briefly before stepping in. "Looks clear."

"A labyrinth," Tad muttered. He shone his light around the other tunnels. "And relying on those two for directions. We're gonna get lost."

Lettie frowned at him. "What's with you?"

"He's always like that," Dieter said.

"Yeah, but he's usually not this vocal about it." Lettie put her hands on her hips and waited.

Tad rolled his eyes. "Those grunts had the right idea. Take off during the night before we all get killed."

"If you want to go back, that's your decision," Gina said, almost hoping he'd take her up on it.

"Then I don't get my credit." He rolled his eyes again. "Come on, let's get lost and get this over with."

Will and Savion led the way down the tunnel. After they'd been walking long enough for Gina's muscles to quiet down their complaints, a flash of red on the wall ahead caught her eye. "What's that?"

Will lifted his secondary light for a better view. A painting of the ruby decorated the side of the tunnel.

"There's another one," Dieter said, pointing further ahead on the opposite wall.

Gina grinned. "I think that means we're going the right way." She glanced at Tad, who still looked unimpressed.

Lettie's response was far more satisfactory. She dug the camera out and dutifully photographed the images as the group continued down the tunnel, bouncing on her toes between each picture. "This is so cool!"

The paintings stopped after a few yards, and the walk became a dull trudge onward once more. Until they came to another triangular passage, this time with five branches.

"What's your book say?" Will asked.

Gina already had it opened to the next step. "Um… Eastward again. And up."

Will checked the tunnels. "All of these lead down. And there are two tunnels leading to the right."

"Up, in this context, would mean inward," Dieter explained. "We want the second from the right."

Will examined the tunnel more briefly this time before proceeding.

Gina sighed as the blank walls passed on either side in an unchanging haze. She'd expected this to be shorter, somehow. Faster. But the ancient Mevoyan culture valued perseverance and endurance. The lengthy trek was probably designed to test those qualities.

More images of rubies signaled they were still on the right track. Lettie responded with equal enthusiasm to last time, but Gina found herself getting impatient. They had the right tunnel. How many more branches before they got to the ruby? Or more writings, or artifacts. Anything significant.

They finally reached the next branching, again with five possible tunnels. Gina found the next image and paused. "Dieter?"

He leaned over her shoulder, one eyebrow raised in wait for her question.

She pointed to the top of the picture, a label above the writing. "Is that 'third' or 'fifth'?"

He opened his mouth, then stopped. "Huh." He took the journal from her and studied the image more closely.

"What's wrong?" Lettie asked.

Gina chewed a hangnail, uncertainty building in her chest. "This image might be the directions for these tunnels, or it might be for the fifth set. It's not clear."

Dieter shook his head and handed the journal back. "It's too degraded. I can't tell."

"Great. We're relying on crappy pictures that can't even show the directions clearly," Tad muttered.

Gina gave him a look. "It's not the picture. The stone this was written on became damaged before it was discovered. We're not sure what caused it." She returned her attention to the image. "If that line is a carved line, then these directions are for this branch. But if it's just a crack, then it's for the fifth one."

"Check the other ones," Dieter suggested. "Maybe the other 'three' or 'five' will be clearer."

Tad snorted and nudged Burke, who just shook his head.

Gina chose to ignore them and focus on the journal instead.

"So why didn't you two figure this out before leading everyone down here?" Burke asked.

"I just noticed that the line could be a crack." Gina found the other image in question. "Crud."

Dieter leaned over her shoulder again. The writing they'd originally interpreted as the directions for the fifth branch were water damaged from a trickle that had made its way into the cave ages ago. Most of the carved symbols were faded, but still readable. Half of the labeling number was gone, though. It was impossible to say for sure if it was a five or a three.

"Oh," he said.

"What's it say?" Lettie asked.

"Uh…" Gina squinted but couldn't make the image any clearer. "I'm not sure."

"Great." Tad drew out the word as if worried that someone might miss the intended sarcasm.

"This is a good moment for a break," Doctor Richards intervened. She set her pack down on the floor. "Have a snack and drink some water."

Will consulted the GPS unit. "It's almost lunchtime anyway. Might as well eat."

The work crew seemed all too happy to comply, chatting and joking amongst themselves as they plopped down and dug out food. Burke sat and ate while still watching Gina and Dieter, his expression that of someone munching popcorn, absorbed in an intriguing show. Lettie ate while standing, hovering.

Dieter nudged Gina. "Eat something. We'll look at it with fresh eyes after we've had some food."

"Sure," she mumbled, still squinting at the image.

He took the journal from her hands and closed it.

She made a face at him, but obediently sat and ate. Her mind whirled through the whole break. Was that line only a crack? What if she led them the wrong way?

Last time she'd messed up, she'd almost gotten everyone killed. A new shiver slipped through her at the thought.

She finished as quickly as possible, then snatched the book back from Dieter and found the two images again. She shone her light from multiple angles but failed to get a better perspective on the line in question. If only she could go back to that cave and look at the image in person again. Then she'd know if it was a line or a crack. Why hadn't she paid better attention when she'd seen it before?

Because she hadn't known that their lives could depend on one single line.

Dieter joined her, brushing crumbs off his hands. "Anything?"

She shook her head.

He studied the images for a few minutes before speaking again. "It looks like a line to me. It's wider than the rest of the crack branching off there."

"You sure?"

"It makes sense. The damage to the rock wall would have occurred at the weaker areas—where the Mevoyan people had chiseled into the walls."

She squinted at the image. It did look like the questionable line narrowed after the place it should have ended. It seemed a reasonable enough explanation. And it fit with their original conclusions, that this was the third direction and the other was the fifth.

"We have it," she said to Will. The others around perked up and listened. A blush threatened her cheeks at the attention. "That is, we're pretty certain we have it. It should be…" She consulted the translation. "North. The middle one."

Will glanced at Dieter, who nodded.

"Load up, slackers," Owen barked to his crew. "We're going."

The crew continued their chatter and jokes while they stood and re-collected the gear.

Tad sighed and hefted his pack. "Time to get lost."

Will leaned closer to Gina. "Does he come with an off switch?"

"If only," Dieter said.

Gina fought a smile and tucked the journal back in her pack. Still, she didn't feel better until the paintings of the ruby appeared a distance down the tunnel, sooner this time than the other two.

"Guess we're on the right path after all." Lettie shot a smug smile at Tad. "I knew they'd figure it out."

"Whatever," he mumbled.

Another timeless walk stretched on. Gina's legs began complaining again. They'd liked the break and preferred immobility to being stretched. She numbly plodded forward, once again feeling impatience grow.

She hadn't realized how thoroughly she was walking on autopilot until she almost walked directly into Savion's back. She backpedaled with a small yelp of surprise.

Will glanced back at her. "You hurt?"

Blushing, she shook her head.

He returned his attention forward. She looked around Savion and realized why they'd stopped.

The dancing light beams from their headlamps zigzagged across a mass of stones filling the tunnel ahead.

"Another cave-in?" Dieter asked.

"All right, grunts," Owen said. "Let's get this clear."

The work crew set their packs down and started forward, but Will held up a hand. "Hang on. This doesn't look like a cave-in."

"Rocks filling a tunnel. Looks like a cave-in to me." Tad stepped closer.

Will looked back at Dieter and Gina. "You said you weren't sure if this is the right one?"

Gina dug out her journal and checked the other image. "If we're wrong, we should have taken the west—I mean, the far left tunnel instead."

He nodded. "We should check that one."

"What makes you think this is the wrong one?" Dieter asked. His tone made it clear he was curious, not doubtful. That was one thing Gina always loved about working with him. He didn't make people feel defensive when he asked questions.

"It doesn't look right." Will shone his light on the chaotic mass of rock.

"It's a bunch of rocks. Blocking a tunnel." Tad aimed his own light toward the ceiling. "Look, you can even see where they fell from. And we saw the paintings of the ruby whatever. You're gonna get us lost."

"I thought that's what you said about this tunnel," Dieter said.

Tad scowled at him and pointed to a nearby painting of the ruby. "You think this is the wrong tunnel?"

"We hired an expert on caves for a reason," Lettie said. "We should listen to him. Maybe the other tunnel has paintings, too."

Gina nodded. "They may have used the paintings as red herrings in false tunnels. If Will says we should check the other tunnel, then it's worth at least taking a look. Better safe than sorry."

"This has already taken forever," Tad grumbled. "Look, we could just get right through and keep going." He reached for a rock.

"Don't!" Gina gasped.

"Stop." Savion's voice echoed in the space.

Tad yanked the rock free.

A scraping noise pierced Gina's eardrums. Metal spikes shot out from cracks in the rock pile. A red-stained edge protruded from Tad's back.

He twitched, then was still.

Dead.

# Chapter 7

Gina screamed, barely hearing her own shocked cry echoed by several of the others.

"Run!" Savion shouted.

A noise ground through the space. She couldn't tell what it was. Couldn't think straight. All she could see were Tad's eyes, fixed open and no longer seeing.

Savion caught her arm and pushed her back along the tunnel. "Run!"

A spike shot out beside her from the middle of one of the ruby paintings. Savion pulled her along just in time to avoid being impaled on another one from the next painting. The grinding noise continued forward.

Her legs finally cooperated, stumbling into a sort of flailing forward momentum. Hot pain shot through her right leg, skin torn by a spike. She shrieked as her legs failed, but Savion's grip on her arm kept her moving forward, almost dragging her as the spikes continued to shoot out just behind her. He ducked under a blade that lashed out just ahead of them.

They were falling behind.

The thought clouded her mind with panic. She grabbed at Savion's arms, willing him to move faster for both their sakes.

He dodged right. Another rusted tip grazed her arm.

"Come on, Gina," Dieter shouted. "Run!"

His voice cut through the terror gripping her. She managed to force her legs into some form of cooperation, pushing herself harder and harder until she only barely lagged behind Savion's longer stride.

More spikes shot out ahead of them. Savion pulled her around one and under another. Someone lay on the ground by the second one. She started to cry out to stop, to go help them back to their feet, but her light caught a flash of glistening red beside the form. Her cry caught in her lungs.

Savion suddenly yanked her forward. It took the last of her strength to keep her feet moving fast enough to avoid falling flat on her face. Dieter caught her before she collapsed to the ground.

Savion stopped beside them, hands on knees, panting. It only took a minute before he straightened to examine a tear in his pack.

It took Gina longer to recover. Her side was enveloped in flames, a pain she couldn't focus on while running but now consumed her attention. She gulped in air and curled over herself, trying to ease the burn.

Doctor Richards pressed some water in her hands and helped her sit before tending to the lacerations on her arm and leg. "Last tetanus shot?"

Gina tried to slow her breathing enough to answer but failed.

"Just before we came down here," Dieter said. "Same as me."

The doctor nodded and sprayed something that stung into the scrape on Gina's arm. She spent more time on the gashed leg. "I'm using skin glue and butterfly bandages, but if you don't take it easy, I may have to resort to stitches." She caught Gina's eye. "So take it easy."

Gina thought she'd be more than happy to comply so long as the expedition allowed for it. It certainly hadn't been her idea to run full-tilt through a homicidal tunnel.

Instant shame and regret stung her mind at the thought. Tad hadn't deserved that.

Her breathing finally slowed back to a more controlled rate. She took another swig of water and turned to Dieter. "Was anyone else hurt?"

He glanced back at the tunnel, a grim look on his face. "A few scrapes and bruises, mostly. But a couple of the workers fell."

The sting sharpened. She looked down.

Dieter put a hand on her shoulder. "It wasn't your fault."

"We were in the wrong tunnel."

"I know."

"If I'd figured out it was just a crack—"

He held up a hand. "We both studied it from every angle possible. We did the best we could. Tad had every warning not to touch those rocks and chose to ignore us. This isn't your fault."

His words made sense to her brain, but wouldn't sink any deeper than that, no matter how hard she tried to push them against the guilt weighing her down.

She turned away, as if doing so physically would help her mind turn away from the guilt as well. She looked over the tunnel they'd fled, finally able to give the spikes a good look. Some were mostly wood with a metal point set in the end, a crude sort of spear. Others were cast in metal the full length. Those ones were more cross-shaped than round, forming four points sticking outward from the center. The lances commonly used by the Mevoyan fighting men. Her hand drifted to the scrape on her arm. Apparently time hadn't dulled the edges enough.

A fuss from the other end of the tunnel's branching space interrupted her thoughts.

"You can't just take off!" Owen's red face looked more purplish under the glare of the LEDs. "You committed to this job, and you're going to see it through!"

Gina found her feet and joined Lettie near the work crew. "What's going on?"

"They want to go back." She gestured to a group of five workers, all of them glaring at Owen.

"We're not sticking around to get drowned or staked," one spat. "We're out of here."

"We will need everyone's assistance," Savion said. "You must stay."

Dieter nudged Gina. "Give me that blank notebook."

She handed it over, not sure his intent. Maybe he'd seen something in the new translations he hoped would persuade the workers to stay.

He opened the journal to a blank page and scribbled a sketch and directions on it, then tore it out and handed it to the spokesman for the group. "Here. I don't want you getting lost on the way back out."

Owen's face darkened. "They can't leave!"

"They've lost their friends. I can't blame them for being afraid the same will happen to them." Dieter turned back to the group. "Feel free to use the room of safety to rest again, but if you light a fire, make sure to extinguish it before you leave. We may need it again."

The spokesman looked calmer at Dieter's words. "We will. Thank you."

"I don't work with quitters." Owen glared at them. "I have a reputation to uphold."

"Consider it untarnished," Dieter said. "Their choice to leave shows that they are not the type of people you want to work with, anyway, so we are all better for it."

Owen looked like he didn't approve of Dieter's brand of logic but couldn't come up with his own logic to respond. He shook his head and stomped a few feet away, where he pretended to be busy with his pack.

The group tried to coax a few other workers to leave with them, but the others shook their head and waved them off. "We knew it was gonna be dangerous when we signed on," Jake said. "You want to leave, then get on with it so the rest of us can get back to work."

"Besides," Burke offered, "the only one dumb enough not to listen isn't going to be a problem anymore."

Gina stared, unable to find her voice. Lettie seemed equally speechless. Dieter and Savion gave the man dark scowls, and Will shook his head. "Not cool, mate."

Doctor Richards looked up from the scrape she was treating and turned a severe look on Burke. "That's hardly appropriate. Go see to those men over there."

Burke shrugged and meandered to the men, looking entirely uninterested in treating their wounds.

The doctor shook her head. "I apologize for his behavior. He's top-notch when it comes to diagnoses and field treatments, which is why I selected him as my assistant. He's always been slightly… lacking in the social graces, but I've never known him to be quite so callous."

"We're all shaken," Dieter said. "I suppose we all have our own ways of dealing with tragedies."

Doctor Richards nodded and returned to her work.

Gina rubbed her forehead. She couldn't help but wonder if the workers that quit had the right idea. She didn't want to see anyone else hurt because of her mistakes.

Dieter handed her the notebook back. "So we're going to the left."

"I guess."

He squeezed her shoulder once more. "We know the right path now. It'll be okay."

She wished she could believe him.

Lettie brushed ineffectively at the dirt on her khaki shorts. "Okay. Before we take one more step, everyone has to promise that if Gina, Dieter, or Will says not to touch something, then you won't touch it. At all. Oh, and Savion, too." She looked around at the others with something that was probably meant to be a fierce, intimidating glare. Her pampered heiress appearance, only slightly disheveled from the journey, made her look like a barking Chihuahua: more cute than intimidating. "Got it?"

"You're the boss," Owen said. The rest of his workers followed his lead in agreement.

"We'll be careful," Doctor Richards promised.

Burke grunted. "I'm not an idiot. Are we just going to stand around doing nothing?"

Will shot a brief frown in his direction but waved them on toward the tunnel on the far left. "Let's go."

Gina pulled out her notebook before slinging her pack onto her back. As they started down the new tunnel, she split her attention between watching the surroundings for signs of danger and searching the writings. She double-checked the next few directions to make sure the translations were clear and accurate. Then she checked for any indicators of potential threats ahead.

About halfway through the tunnel, she glanced up and flinched at the sight of a painting of the ruby. She had to convince her heart to calm down, that no lances or spears were coming out of the painting. They were in the right tunnel this time. Safe. It still took some work to convince herself of that, though.

They reached the next branch before she'd finished her check through the notebook. This one was less like a triangular shape and more like a hub. The rounded ceiling rose high above them, and as she slowly turned to take it in, she counted about nine different openings, not counting the one they'd come down. Each were like all the ones they'd seen so far, with paved cobblestone floors and no markings to distinguish one from the next.

Will pulled out something that looked like a fat marker and swiped it on the wall beside the exit of their tunnel. It sparkled in the LED lights. "In case we need help finding our way back."

Smart move, Gina realized. In the other branches, the new tunnels had generally led away from the exiting tunnel, making it fairly easy to identify the way back. In this hub, several of the new branches looked like they headed back the same direction as the tunnel they were in. If they had to leave the way they came, this would make it easier to retrace their steps.

"Which way now?" Lettie asked, craning her neck toward the journal open in Gina's hands.

Dieter stepped beside Gina and looked over her shoulder. "Now I see why the directions for this one were so complex."

She dug through the pages to find the directions for the fourth branching. "East with a rise, counting of the sun, number of the ruby."

Lettie gave her a blank look, as did most of the others.

"One step at a time." Dieter stood in the mouth of the tunnel they'd come from, facing forward, and walked straight to the center of the hub. Then he turned directly right and pointed to the tunnels he faced. "East."

"With a rise," Gina said, joining him in the middle. Two tunnels were close enough to centered that either could be considered the 'east' tunnel, but one gradually sloped upwards while the other sloped down. She pointed to the one that sloped upwards. "That's our reference."

"What's 'counting of the sun' supposed to mean?" Lettie asked.

"The Mevoyan people were far enough south that the sun usually curved slightly northward," Dieter explained. "So the sun seemed to follow a skewed arc from right to left."

"And we count the number of the ruby," Gina said.

"What's that?" Will asked.

"Three," Gina and Dieter said in unison. Gina blushed, ducked her head, and motioned for Dieter to continue.

"Three was a sacred number in their culture. The number was used in conjunction to references to the ruby on multiple occasions." He pointed to the 'east' tunnel once more, then counted three tunnels to the left. "That's the correct tunnel."

"You guys are sure this time?" Burke asked.

Doctor Richards shushed him.

Dieter started forward, but Gina held back, checking over the translation once more.

He looked back at her. "Gina…"

"It can't hurt to be sure." She carefully retraced their steps, finding the east tunnel, then counting from it to the correct path. "Okay. It's that way."

The hubs grew increasingly larger and more complex, some even containing more than one level. Each time, Gina double- or triple-checked the writings before letting the group move on. But as the hours passed with no further problems, she double-checked less frequently, only verifying a word here or a direction there. She was starting to feel better, more confident. They were going the right way. Maybe they'd even find the gem before the day ended.

They paused for lunch after hours of walking. Gina wanted to push forward, but when she reluctantly sat, her feet and legs issued celebratory messages of gratitude. She hadn't realized just how long they'd been at it and how sore she'd gotten until they stopped.

"I didn't realize how big the cave would be," she said, rubbing at an aching muscle. "I'd have started walking more to prepare if I'd known."

"Yeah, it's different than I thought it'd be," Lettie agreed. "Kind of more boring, too."

Gina glanced at her friend, but kept her mouth shut.

Burke wasn't quite so reserved. "Sorry to hear that almost getting killed twice is too boring for you."

"That's not what I meant." Lettie frowned at him. "I just didn't expect there would be so much walking without anything going on. I thought there would be… I don't know, um…"

"Boulders falling from the ceiling, rooms filled with snakes and skeletons, maybe some Nazis chasing you?" Burke said.

His sarcastic summary of Indiana Jones seemed to go right over Lettie's head. "Yeah, kind of, except maybe not the Nazi part. They aren't around anymore."

Burke snorted.

Dieter had to give Gina a hand up to get off the floor. She winced as her legs and feet joined in immediate protests against the too-soon movement. "Ooh."

"We're a good way through the labyrinth," he said. "With any hope, we'll find the ruby shortly after we finish."

The next tunnel was easy to identify, and the group set off down it. To Gina's relief, the number of branches began to decrease once more after that, making it easier and easier to be sure they had the right way. She barely flipped through the journal except when they reached the hubs, instead focusing on keeping pace and not letting her protesting limbs slow the group down.

The tunnels began a steady descent, making it a bit easier on her legs. The hours melted past as they made their way through hub after hub. Gina felt weariness beginning to tug at her by the time they reached the last hub. Thankfully, there were only two tunnels branching away from that one.

She checked the directions and pointed to the one on the right before Dieter had a chance to look with her. "That one."

"You sure?" Burke asked.

Dieter looked at the page and nodded. "It's that one." He glanced up at her. "We're almost through."

She managed a tired smile. Hopefully the tunnel would emerge into the room with the pool. Otherwise, they might have to stop for another night's rest there in the caves. She'd questioned Lettie's decision to bring so many extra supplies—water and food for several days, extra batteries for the lights, and so on—but now she realized how smart her friend had been. Still, she found herself growing more and more anxious to find their goal and return to daylight and fresh air.

The tunnel proved much longer than the others. Gina was almost ready to collapse by the time they reached the end.

"This can't be right," Will said, slowing. He shone his light around the space.

The tunnel ended in another hub shape, a rounded room with a high ceiling. It was only about fifteen feet in width and length, forming a near-perfect circle. And there were no other exits.

"So it's the other tunnel." Burke turned around.

"No, this is the right tunnel." Dieter slowly surveyed the space. His light illuminated faint, worn-down words etched into stones in the solid rock wall. The wall had been broken in a few places, and stones jutted out from those spots. Buttons and levers. The ceiling was decorated with various paintings, but none looked like the ruby. A bird here, a cloud there, the sun in the middle, and various sacred images were all she saw.

Gina pulled the journal back out of her pack and began hunting for answers.

"It's a dead end," Burke pressed. "You got the wrong tunnel."

Dieter gave Burke a look from where he crouched by one of the etchings. "We have the correct tunnel. We merely need to determine the way onward from here."

"Remember, that closure room thing didn't have an exit, not until they found the right stones to press," Lettie said.

"And we all remember how well that worked."

A flash of irritation battled the automatic shame that washed through Gina's mind. She kept her eyes on the notebook. "We'll get it right this time."

"Sure you will."

Savion stepped in front of Burke, towering over the man. He'd been so quiet that Gina had almost forgotten he was there. The fierce look on his face gave her a quick reminder of why she felt so intimidated by him.

"Let them work," he said, his deep voice ringing in the space.

Burke hesitated, then backed off.

"Thank you." Dieter beckoned Gina. "I think these are directions, but I'm having trouble making them out."

A few loose pebbles rattled away from her feet as she crossed to his side and crouched to see the inscription, adding her light to his. "It's really faded. Let's see… that first one looks like 'anchor,' I think."

"That's what I thought. Can you make out the next one?"

Will set down his pack and sat, pulling out some food to munch on while he waited. The rest of the group followed his lead. Lettie stayed close, first taking pictures and then holding her light high to help illuminate their work, but the others found places to sit.

A yelp from behind her yanked Gina's attention to the other side of the space. The skinny worker, Shrimpy, flailed, his feet sliding on some loose rocks. He pitched sideways and barely caught himself on one of the protruding stones.

No one moved for a moment, but nothing seemed to happen.

"You hurt?" Owen asked.

Shrimpy shook his head, red-faced.

"Then sit down and quit acting like a clown."

He obediently straightened.

The rock lever shifted as soon as his weight came off it. A grinding sound rumbled further down the tunnel they'd come from.

Lettie yelped and skittered to the back of the space, standing on her tiptoes to see. Dieter maneuvered Gina behind him, slightly crouched and braced for something to happen.

An almost solid wall of stench flooded the space.

Gina gasped and gagged, coughing and frantically pressing her hand over her nose. Her eyes watered and stung.

"Gas?" Burke frantically waved at the air in front of him.

Savion shook his head. "Death."

"We're going to die?" Lettie squeaked.

Savion eyed her. "No. It is the smell of something that has died."

Gina's panic slowly eased at his words. The smell wasn't necessarily a trap. Maybe they'd opened a ceremonial tomb of sorts.

"I'll check it out," Will volunteered. "You stay here and try to figure out what that wall says."

Dieter nodded and returned his attention to the inscription.

Savion followed Will, along with Owen, Shrimpy, and Petty.

Gina turned back to the wall, feeling a bit better. Will and Savion would recognize any threats. And they'd let her and Dieter know if they found anything significant. It was fine. She and Dieter resumed their work together, carefully examining the faded writing and struggling to get an accurate transcription written down.

"There's an exit here," she said, scanning the part they'd already copied. "We should find a hidden latch in a stone. We just have to reach in and pull to open the door."

Burke's eyes slid around the room with minimal interest. "So where's this latch?"

"I'm not sure. We've still got three more words to go." She pointed to the next one. "Is that part a crack or a line?"

"Not that again," Burke muttered.

"Quiet down and let them work," Doctor Richards scolded.

A shout rang from down the tunnel. Gina jumped and whirled around. The remaining workers scrambled to the tunnel entrance, shining their lights to see what was happening.

Lights bobbed frantically far down the tunnel. The men who'd gone to investigate came into view of their lights, running at top speed toward them.

"Get back! Go!" Owen yelled.

Movement writhed behind the runners, low to the ground. Gina couldn't make out what it was. She backed up cautiously, moving slowly with the others, still trying to make out the approaching danger.

A flash of green scales. A claw. Gina's breath caught. The men were being chased by animals, some sort of lizard, from the looks of it. They were big for lizards, almost the size of a small dog, but longer with their tails.

Lettie let out a squeak, apparently seeing the same thing. "Faster! Get in here!"

Gina's eyes searched the hub. No exit. No door. How would they get out before the lizards reached them? The stench seemed to grow stronger as the lizards drew closer. The smell of death.

The creatures snapped and hissed at the fleeing men, darting forward in sharp lunges. One of them caught Petty by the ankle. He shouted and stumbled, falling flat onto the cobblestone almost a hundred yards from the hub. The mass swarmed over him.

"Get up," Lettie cried. "Come on, you can do it!"

Shrimpy kept running full-tilt, but Owen, Will, and Savion slowed, turning to help.

Petty screamed and twisted under the churning pile of flicking tails and slashing claws. Then his screams fell silent.

Savion shoved Owen and Will. "Go. Run!"

They obeyed without further order, Savion right behind them.

The creatures disentangled themselves from the mass. Gina saw red. On the floor, on their mouths, on their claws. Too much red. Her stomach churned. Her feet stumbled backwards.

The lizards hissed and darted forward again.

# Chapter 8

Dieter caught Gina's arm and pulled her back to the inscription. "We have to find that door. Now."

She stared at the faint etchings without comprehending. Lettie was screaming. Someone else was shouting. It all flooded her system with terrified confusion.

"This word, can you make it out?" Dieter pressed, pointing.

She couldn't. Couldn't stay here. Had to go. Her chest tightened until she couldn't breathe.

Dieter grunted something she didn't understand and hastily worked to copy down the last words. "Gina, I need you to help me with this one. I can't make it out." He grabbed her arm and pulled her closer.

Someone shouted just behind her. She heard a crunching sound. A tail flicked her arm. She screamed and backpedaled.

A lizard hissed at her. Darted forward.

Dieter kicked it, knocking it away. "Come on, Gina!"

Another lizard scurried forward, red dripping from its mouth.

She couldn't breathe. Couldn't move.

Savion stepped between her and the lizard. Swung his pack and sent it flying. Turned to her. His face hovered inches from hers, his eyes intense and locked with her own.

"You are needed. You must dismiss the fear."

His voice thundered through her ears, blocking out the other cries and thuds and scuffling sounds.

Her chest unlocked. She could breathe.

"Here, this word." Dieter pulled her back to the wall and pointed.

Savion stayed in place behind her, using his pack, feet, and fists to keep the lizards away from her and Dieter.

Gina took a deep breath. She could do this. She had to.

She crouched beside the inscription and shone her light on it from one angle, then another. "That line looks like a crack. This is 'cloud.' I think."

"Then the last phrase is 'have a vision in the clouds.'"

Something hit her leg. She shrieked and stumbled back.

Savion grabbed the lizard and threw it. She could see now that there were too many. Everyone but her, Dieter, and Lettie fought for their lives at the tunnel entrance, but more lizards made their way through, and the mass kept forcing the fighters back inch by inch. Soon, they'd be overwhelmed by the creatures.

"Hurry," Dieter said, pulling her attention back to the inscription. "Find the door, and we're all saved. We can block up the doorway. Maybe even close it behind us. But we have to find it, now!"

Saved. She had to do this. She looked at the words. Her voice shook as badly as her body, but she managed to focus enough to translate. "That word isn't 'vision.' It's more like 'look.'"

"Look in the clouds," he translated.

"Up." She shone her lantern upwards, illuminating the painting of the cloud she'd seen before. It was on the side of the cave wall, at least twelve feet up.

Dieter looked around. "Will, get over here!"

Will managed to fight back a snapping lizard and escape to join them behind the mass of fighters.

Dieter pointed to the cloud painting. "There's a latch hidden behind that cloud. Can you reach it?"

Will eyed the image for a moment, his headlamp light flicking over it. "I need a boost."

They hurried underneath it, Lettie cringing beside them, and crouched to boost him up.

A lizard clamped onto Gina's wrist.

She screamed and fell over backwards, wildly flailing her arm to try to shake it off.

Dieter caught her and pulled her back to her feet before more lizards could swarm her. He punched the lizard until it dropped.

Another one lunged at her, and she barely managed to kick before it caught her ankle. It hissed and lunged a different direction, striking at Lettie.

Savion grabbed it and threw it down the tunnel. "Quickly." He put meaty hands on Will and hefted him up.

Will scrambled onto Savion's shoulders like a child and stood. He felt around the cloud image, searching for the hidden latch.

Dieter pushed Gina back and kicked a lizard she hadn't realized was there. She yelped and scooted back further against the wall, only barely remembering to make sure she didn't run into any buttons or levers.

The others kept inching closer to them, forced back by the swarm. "Come on, get it already!" Burke shouted.

"Watch your left," Owen barked.

Burke spun and lashed out at a lizard before it caught him. "Hurry up!"

Owen swung his pack and sent three flying at once. "Shut up and let them work."

"Got it!" Will shouted. His hand disappeared into the wall. A grinding noise preceded a rumble above their heads.

Gina's breath caught. Was the ceiling going to fall on them? Had she gotten the translation wrong?

A dark opening appeared above them, right beside Will. He whooped and caught the edges, pulling himself in with ease. A moment later, a rope dropped from the inky hole. "Climb up, hurry!"

Dieter pushed Gina to the rope. Before she could start climbing, Savion grabbed her like he'd done with Will and pushed her up toward the opening. Will caught her wrists and pulled her in. She quickly turned and reached down a hand to help the next person up.

Dieter reached for Lettie. A lizard shot past him and latched onto her ankle. She fell down, shrieking.

Burke climbed up the rope and hollered back at the others, "Get moving already!"

Doctor Richards reached Lettie at the same time as Dieter. The doctor pulled her up while Dieter knocked the lizard away. Lettie could barely stand, sobbing and shrieking in frantic terror.

Lich and Shrimpy climbed hastily. Gina helped Shrimpy over the ledge, then Will pulled Lich up.

Dieter pulled Lettie toward the rope. "Get up, Savion. We've got her."

Savion paused, then climbed quickly. He ignored the offered hands, swinging up onto the ledge with almost as much ease as Will. He stood in Gina's way, reaching down toward the others.

She backed off, holding her light high to help the others see as they climbed.

Jake reached the top. Owen stayed put beside Dieter, fighting the lizards back so the doctor and Lettie could reach the rope.

Doctor Richards pushed Lettie forward, but Lettie just kept flailing, sobbing and struggling wildly.

"Lettie," Gina shouted, hoping her voice would get through to her friend. "It's safe up here. Climb!"

Lettie sobbed and stumbled over herself.

Dieter staggered backwards, a lizard on his leg. Owen caught his arm before he fell.

"Savion," Doctor Richards called. She grabbed Lettie around the waist, crouched, and pushed up with all her might.

Savion caught Lettie's waving arm and pulled. Lettie tumbled over the ledge and curled up into a ball, weeping.

A flash of movement caught Gina's eye from below.

"Look out!" Savion shouted.

Three lizards slammed into Doctor Richards. She fell.

"Get her and get up here," Will called down. "Hurry!"

Dieter managed to shake off the lizard and turned to the doctor.

The swarm had already found her. Her screams filled the space for a moment before cutting off sharply.

Owen caught Dieter's arm and pushed him toward the rope, away from the doctor.

Gina wanted to scream. No, you can't leave her. You have to help her. You can't just let her die.

The lizards turned their attention to Owen and Dieter. They hissed. Crouched. Lunged.

Owen kicked the first few aside and pushed Dieter upward. Savion caught Dieter's arm and hauled him up. Owen jumped onto the rope behind him, kicked off a lizard that tried to catch his leg, and climbed until Will could catch him and help him the rest of the way.

Gina's voice finally returned to her. "The doctor… we can't…"

Will pulled the rope up while Owen swung his pack at the lizards. They were trying to climb. Their claws scraped against the wall below.

Savion pushed the massive rock panel that had sealed the entrance before. Leaned his shoulder into it. It shifted forward with a grinding sound.

Panic bubbled in Gina's chest. "We can't just leave her!" Her feet cooperated enough to stumble forward.

Dieter caught her shoulder. Held her back.

"We can't!" She struggled to get free, but his grip remained firm.

The rock panel settled back in place with a thud. The hissing sounds fell silent.

Tears slid down Gina's cheeks without a sound. She dropped to the rock floor, unable to do anything but tremble and cry.

Burke straightened, his expression strangely distant and professional. "I need to treat those bites before they get infected."

Gina barely noticed as he made his way around the room, identifying the worst injuries, cleaning wounds, and administering antibiotics. She barely noticed when he tended to her wrist, leaving it wrapped in a large bandage. Or when he checked the older cut on her leg, applied more antibiotic cream, and covered it with fresh wrapping.

Dieter sat down beside her, his own wounds already dressed. "It was too late."

She knew that. She didn't want to, but she did.

"We did what we could."

She looked away. "We should go back. Leave before anyone else gets hurt." Her voice sounded thin.

He motioned to the closed door. "That's the only way back. Those creatures are still down there. We can't go that way now." He put a hand on her arm until she looked at him. "The only way is forward."

New tears escaped her eyes.

He hesitated, then awkwardly wrapped an arm across her shoulders. She tried to swallow her emotions, to stay strong. The tears won in the end. She turned to him and wept.

She didn't feel much better for it afterwards, sitting up and drying her face.

He handed her a dirty cloth. "Sorry. It's all I have."

She nodded her thanks and dried her face, then blew her nose.

Lettie crawled over from where she'd been curled up in the middle of the floor and leaned against her other side. "I'm sorry. I don't know why, I just sort of… freaked out."

"It happens." Gina hadn't been much help, either. Despite her earlier resolve to be stronger and not panic. She sighed.

"I didn't," Lettie started, but paused. "I guess… I thought it'd be different. I didn't realize…"

Gina wrapped an arm around her friend, understanding. They sat in silence for a while. Gina's eyes finally wandered the room, taking in the space they'd found. It was smaller than the round room they'd left, more oblong and natural. Nothing jutted from or etched into the walls here, and like the tunnel walls, only a few tool marks showed where the room had been shaped. It was smaller than the Room of Safety and didn't have all the supplies, but it seemed to serve a similar purpose: a large place for weary travelers to rest. On the wall opposite the door they'd come through, a dark tunnel led further into the caves.

Will crossed the space and sat down beside them. "We lost a few of the workers back there, as well as the doctor. I think we need to focus on finding a way out."

A new shudder crept through Gina. She'd seen Petty fall. Apparently some of the others had been lost, too. She looked around and realized only four members of the work crew remained. Owen, Jake, Shrimpy, and Lich. The rest had all been lost, aside from the small group that had gone back on their own. Because of the dangers. Guilt and responsibility settled like a weight on Gina's chest.

"The only way out is forward," Dieter said.

"Unless we find another place the tunnels branch. The wrong tunnels might not all be traps. Some might lead out."

Dieter glanced at Gina, then nodded. "Very well. If we find another wrong tunnel, we can check to see if it's an exit."

"Sure, if you want their deaths to mean nothing," Burke said.

They looked at him.

He gave them a 'duh' look. "They came because they thought we could find the ruby. I think it's pretty obvious they knew they could get killed. If they didn't when we started, they figured it out pretty quickly. Or did you forget our little swim?"

Owen frowned at him.

"I'm just saying, they knew it was dangerous and stuck with it anyway. We leave now, then they died for nothing." He turned to his pack and put his medical equipment away. "If you find an exit and want to ditch, go for it. I just thought you guys believed in finding this thing."

The room remained silent for a long time.

Will exhaled. "It's late. Let's get some rest. We can start again in the morning."

Scaled monsters with rusted metal claws and ruby eyes chased Gina through dream after dream. Her screams fell mutely from her mouth, though she tried harder and harder until she finally heard a scream fill the air.

Her eyes flew open at the second scream. She sat up and blinked the sleep away in the dim light coming from the one lantern Will had left on near the wall.

Others sat up, too. Owen jumped to his feet, looking around in sleep-bleared confusion. "Wha's goin' on?"

Lettie stumbled into the room from the tunnel, her face pale. A trembling finger pointed back the way she'd come. "It—there's—body!"

Dieter fluidly rose from his sleeping bag on the other side of Gina. He flicked on his light and aimed it at the tunnel. "A body?"

Savion raised an eyebrow. "A skeleton, from previous travelers."

Lettie shook her head frantically, unintelligible sounds emitting from her mouth.

Gina kicked free of her sleeping bag and went to her friend's side, holding her shoulders. "What was it?"

Lettie's shaking finger moved from pointing at the tunnel to pointing at the floor. An empty sleeping bag lay between Owen and Shrimpy.

Owen's eyes narrowed as the last of the sleep fog left him. "Jake?"

Lettie whimpered.

Savion and Dieter already strode toward the tunnel, Savion turning his own light on. Owen followed just a step behind.

Gina craned her neck. Part of her wanted to look and see, to see that it was all some sort of mistake. Lettie had a bad dream and thought she'd seen something. Or maybe it was a sick sort of prank. There couldn't be a body.

But the nauseated feeling in her stomach said she was grasping at straws.

Owen's voice flew back to them with a crude exclamation. He thundered back to the room and grabbed Lettie's arm. "What happened? What did you see?"

Lettie gasped and let out a wail.

Dieter quietly removed Owen's hand and pushed him a step back. "Tell us what you saw, Lettie."

It took a moment for the whimpering sounds to turn into words. "I—I woke up. I thought I heard something, and I saw something moving in the tunnel. I went to see, and…" She shuddered. Tears glistened in the dim light.

The others filed into the tunnel, curiosity driving them to see the details for themselves. Gina finally gave in and took a couple of steps into the tunnel, craning her neck to see.

Her stomach lurched and threatened to empty when she saw it. The worker lay toward the left wall of the tunnel just a few yards in. His body twisted in unnatural shapes, and most of the flesh was gone. Long gashes cut through what skin remained.

She stumbled back from the sight, pressing a hand over her mouth to fend off the rising bile.

Lettie caught Dieter's arm. "It's the lizards!" she whispered. "They found a way to get us. They're going to kill the rest of us!"

"This wasn't one of the lizards," Burke said, squinting at the corpse. "The claw marks are too deep."

Gina's stomach twisted again.

"Then what did this?" Lich demanded.

Savion shone his light further down the tunnel. "I will see."

Dieter put Lettie's hand in Gina's. "Stay put. We'll be right back."

Owen went with the two, their lights bobbing and disappearing further down the tunnel.

Gina's fingers tightened on Lettie's. Last time the men had gone to investigate something...

But the lights came bobbing back before long. Owen shook his head as he approached. "There's nothing down there. Just a door, and it hasn't been opened in ages."

"Then..." Burke looked around. "There's just us."

No one spoke for a minute.

Lettie looked around, eyes wide. "No one here did this. They couldn't. It's... They couldn't!"

Will folded his arms and shifted his weight from one leg to the other, looking uncomfortable. "I've seen claw marks like that before."

"Where?" Owen demanded. "What did this?"

"I was backpacking with a friend through Colorado. It was pretty secluded. He got a ways ahead of me around a bend. When I caught up, he was…" He looked away.

"What was it?" Owen pressed.

Will took a deep breath. "An Ondier."

# Chapter 9

Lettie squeaked.

Gina gasped. Fear slipped through her in a cold chill. An Ondier? Here, with them? Her eyes darted around. It couldn't be. It wasn't possible.

Owen frowned at Will. "You want us to believe there's an Ondier here? They're practically extinct. How would one end up with us?"

Will put his hands up in a placating gesture. "All I'm saying is, those claw marks look exactly like what I saw on my friend." He looked around, and Gina saw fear lurking behind his eyes. Fear and suspicion.

Her own gaze echoed his, seeking out each face around her. The same fear and suspicion reflected in their eyes, and she was sure it was in hers, too. She couldn't believe it, couldn't bring herself to accept or even consciously acknowledge the possibility. Yet her mind kept whispering at her with each face she saw. Burke certainly had the cold personality. He didn't look that strong, though. No, an Ondier in disguise wouldn't necessarily look strong. It could be any of them. Could it be Owen? Lich? Savion? His closed-off stare was as intimidating as when she first saw it.

She shivered.

Owen glared at Burke. "If there really is an Ondier here, I think we all know who it is."

Burke returned the glare. "Sure. Big, burly meathead—you're just the type."

"But it can't be," Lettie said, her voice barely audible. "There can't be one here."

"It could be anyone," Lich said. Her narrowed gaze passed over the circle of people. She jerked her head toward Will. "Could even be beanpole here."

"I'm the one who said it might be an Ondier," Will said. "If it was me, why would I draw attention to myself?"

"For that exact reason," Owen said, folding his arms. "So you could make yourself look innocent."

"This is getting us nowhere," Savion said.

Burke flicked a look in the massive man's direction. His fingers wrapped around his pack like a weapon. "What about you? Mr. Jungle Man, living away from society? Wouldn't be hard to hide your true nature that way, would it?"

Dieter caught Gina and Lettie by the arms, pushing them behind himself. "Stay back and remain quiet," he said quietly, never taking his eyes off the tense conflict dominating the room.

"You seem awful eager to point the blame somewhere other than yourself." Owen pulled out one of the rock axes and hefted it in his hands like a bat, eyes fixed on Burke.

Will put a hand up. "There's no need for that, Owen."

"Speaking of people who are eager to point blame elsewhere." Burke returned Owen's glare, hefting his pack higher.

"That's enough," Dieter barked out. "Put the weapons down. Savion's right. This isn't helping."

"You took your sweet time speaking up," Shrimpy snapped. "Trying to blend in the background and hide who you are? It could be you just as much as anyone else!"

"You're right," Dieter said.

The others paused and stared.

"You're absolutely right," he continued. "It could be me. Or it could be Will. Or Owen. Or even Lettie or Gina. We have no way of knowing for sure who it is. If you guys want to start attacking each other and fighting, you might wind up finding the Ondier. But most likely, we'll end up with a bunch of dead humans, innocent people, and their blood on your hands." He met eyes with the others in turn, his expression calm and authoritative.

Some of the others defiantly held his gaze for a moment, but eventually broke eye contact.

"We know there might be an Ondier here. It's good to be aware and cautious, but there's no call to overreact and panic. We're watching now. Whoever it is will have a harder time acting after this. And if they do, we'll catch them before they get too far."

Gina glanced around at the rest of the people in the cave, unconsciously chewing a hangnail. Owen and Burke still had angry expressions, but she could see that Dieter's words were getting through even to them.

"We're all exhausted and scared. There's no way we can all think clearly in this state. We need to rest."

"So the Ondier can shred us in our sleep?" Burke snorted. "No, thanks."

Dieter eyed him, thinking. "Statistically, there are so few Ondier left that there couldn't possibly be more than one with us, if there really is one at all. We'll keep two people on watch at all times. If the Ondier tries anything again, at least one person will be able to sound the alarm. I'd be willing to take part in the first watch."

Will seemed content at the idea, but Burke and Owen continued scowling.

"I'm not about to sleep now. You lot would probably let it eat me," Burke said.

"I ain't sleeping, either," Shrimpy said.

Lich folded her arms. "I'm with Shrimpy."

"Ditto," Owen said. He nudged Lich. "Let's see what we can do to give Jake some honor." The two of them disappeared down the tunnel.

Gina felt ill again.

Dieter shrugged. "If all of you are staying awake, that's more than enough for the first watch. I'll get some rest, then." He climbed back into his sleeping bag.

Lettie looked at Gina like a headlight-stricken deer. "I don't think I can sleep after that. I don't think I'll be able to sleep ever again."

Gina gave another peek around the room. Will had bunked down, as had Savion, but Burke and Shrimpy remained sitting up, holding various items like weapons, glaring suspiciously at each other. She had a feeling that when Owen and Lich returned, they'd do the same. She sighed. "I don't think I'll be able to sleep, either. But we should at least try."

After Gina climbed back into her sleeping bag, she tried to close her eyes and fall asleep, but it eluded her. She kept seeing images of the gashed skin of the dead worker, drawings and blurred photographs from old textbook lessons about the Ondier, the homicidal look in her companions' eyes when they heard an Ondier might be among them.

She must have finally given in to her exhaustion, though, because the next thing she knew, she woke up to find the cave only lit by one lantern. Lettie, Will, and Shrimpy all slept soundly in their sleeping bags. Burke snored from a half-upright position against the wall. Owen and Lich were also fast asleep while still sitting, propped up against each other.

Savion sat with eyes faintly reflected in the lantern's light. Gina's heart jumped, but then she realized he must have been keeping watch. Only him? A movement beside her drew her attention to Dieter. He also sat, leafing through their journal of notes. He glanced at her. "Sleep well?"

"No." She felt like she hadn't slept at all. Everything hurt. "You keeping watch?"

"Yes. In honesty, I wasn't able to sleep when I tried. I thought I might review what we've learned."

She sat up and rubbed the sleep crust away from her eyes. "What time is it?"

"Time to wake," Savion said. He reached over and nudged Owen.

Owen was on his feet in a second, rock axe over his head in preparation to strike. Lich fell backwards with a shriek and jumped to her own feet with only slightly less speed. Burke yelped and jerked, flailing his arms against the wall behind him.

Will and Lettie sat bolt upright. "What is it? Did it attack?" Lettie squeaked.

Dieter exhaled and set the journal aside. "No one's attacking. It's just time to wake up."

Burke's chest heaved, his eyes still wide. "Heck of a way to wake us."

"I did not intend to startle," Savion said.

Owen lowered the axe. "You wanna give me a little more warning before you go shoving me next time? Give me a—"

Lich shoved him before he could finish his statement. "Nice reflexes, smooth guy. You gonna wet yourself over every little bump now?"

Will stretched and disentangled himself from his sleeping bag. "Come on. Let's load up and move on."

Owen glanced down at Shrimpy. Amazingly, the man was still fast asleep in the folds of his bag. Owen rolled his eyes. "Could sleep through a train wreck." He gave Shrimpy a kick. "Get up, lazy. We're moving."

Shrimpy scrambled upright, sleeping bag still wrapped around half his body, expression wild from his sudden awakening. "I wasn't asleep."

Gina shook her head in wonder and turned her attention to packing away her things. She still didn't know how she'd managed to sleep at all, as poor as it had been. Part of her almost wished she could be like Shrimpy and enjoy being oblivious a bit longer.

The group remained quiet and subdued through breakfast, most still casting suspicious glances around at the others. Lich only ate a couple bites before tossing the rest of her food pack aside, a look of disgust on her face. Gina couldn't quite tell if the woman's appetite had been put off by the previous day's events or if she just couldn't stand the cardboard-esque rations any longer. Or if it was something else. If the Ondier had just eaten last night, would it be hungry again so soon? Gina shuddered at the thought.

Savion and Dieter seemed to be the only ones disinterested in the witch hunt. Gina tried to keep her eyes forward and not worry about it, but creeping fears kept her glancing over her shoulder at every little movement.

They proceeded into the tunnel. Gina did her best not to look at the blood smears on the walls. A mound of carefully stacked rocks marked the place Jake had fallen. It was the closest they could come to a burial in the stark rock caves. Will and Shrimpy both crossed themselves as they passed the makeshift grave. Owen gave a little salute of sorts, and Lich thumped a fist against her chest a couple times.

Gina walked on, feeling a little guilty she hadn't made any gesture herself. It was her expedition, after all. It didn't matter that she hadn't really known the guy. She'd been at least partially responsible for his death. She looked back, wishing there was something she could do or say that would ease the pang in her conscience.

Dieter gently guided her onward. "There's nothing you could have done."

He'd misunderstood her look, but she let it go. "We'll find it, right?"

He looked at her with a question mark in his eyes.

"Because then this wouldn't be for nothing."

Understanding passed over his face, and he nodded. "We'll find it."

"We reached the door," Will called.

Gina moved forward with Dieter behind her. This door had clear lines around the edges, unlike all the hidden doors they'd encountered before. "I wonder why they made this one so obvious."

Dieter pointed to carved words in the stone above the door. "Let's find out."

It only took a few minutes of work to translate the short message. It provided a few warnings they'd already seen in other writings—the dangerous powers of the ruby, and how only the pure of heart would be righteous enough to wield it, and the like. The rest was fairly straightforward.

"If you are prepared for clean, the door opens to the east," Dieter read.

"Purity, not clean. I think it means that if you're ready and pure, then you can open the door…" Gina peered at the right side of the door and spotted a small hole. She shone her light inside, spotted nothing untoward, and reached in. Her fingers landed on a small latch, which she pulled.

The door groaned, then rumbled aside.

She smiled. "To the east. The right."

"What's that part about being pure?" Owen frowned.

"Ritual purification was very important to the Mevoyan people," Gina explained. "It was expected that anyone wanting to enter a sacred place would go through special washing and ritual procedures to make sure they were 'pure.' The door was just saying that any Mevoyan person expecting to enter the chamber with the ruby would have to participate in those rituals before getting this far." A light of excitement cut through the cloud of fear and guilt that had been following her. She looked at Dieter. "That means we're close, right? It must!"

"It's likely." His expression remained reserved, but she could see a new sparkle hiding behind his solemnity. "We won't know for sure until we find the pool, though."

"So what about this purity thing?" Lettie asked. "Should we wash our hands or something before we keep going?"

Gina couldn't help a small smile. "The words are just instructions for their people."

"But if there's a trap…"

"Right," Burke said. "Because a trap made hundreds of years ago can magically tell if you've used your Purell or not."

Lettie gave him a look.

"I don't think they could have made a trap to determine whether the rituals were followed," Gina said. "We should be safe to continue."

"On we go, then." Will stepped through the door, Savion once again at his side.

The doorway appeared to open on a dead end, but a blind tunnel intersected to the right. It rose even higher than the other tunnels, and while all the tunnels they'd passed through before followed natural twists and turns throughout, this one remained arrow-straight as far as Gina could see. It was also slightly wider than the other tunnels, and shallow ledges stuck out from the wall on the left side. The lengths varied, as did their height along the tunnel wall. Some were at a comfortable counter height, others closer to eye height, and a few even rested down near their shins.

"What are those for?" Burke asked.

Gina dug out the journal and flipped through, but she already knew she wouldn't find anything. She couldn't remember a single word in any of the writings about a long tunnel with ledges like this.

Dieter looked over her shoulder, then shook his head. "I'm not sure."

"Me neither," Gina confessed. She bent slightly to see underneath one of the higher ones. A small, black gap rested just beneath it. "They may be levers."

"So don't touch," Will interpreted. "Got it."

He stepped forward, but Gina stayed put, studying the ledges. "Wait."

"What now?" Burke grunted.

"Bug off and let the girl work," Lich snapped.

"You wanna start something?" he returned, scowling at her.

"Silence." Savion's voice echoed slightly in the long tunnel.

Dieter eyed Gina. "What is it?"

She ran her fingers lightly over the closest ledge. Peered underneath. "The purity rituals."

Dieter's gaze flicked down the tunnel. "You think these were for the purification?"

"The words outside the door could have meant 'prepared to become pure' instead of 'ready and pure' like we thought. If that's the case, there would have been pressure on these slabs as the Mevoyan entrant underwent the rituals."

"Which would have moved the ledge downward." He stared at her. "They did come up with a way to determine if the rituals had been followed."

"So you think we need to put something on these ledges?" Will asked.

Gina nodded. "It makes sense."

"And if you're wrong, you're going to push on all those ledges and get us killed," Burke said.

"If we're right, but try to proceed without touching the ledges, we could trigger a trap anyway," Dieter said. "I believe Gina's correct. These ledges were for the purification rituals, and if they aren't used, we may not be able to proceed."

Burke muttered something else, but it was too quiet to hear clearly.

Lettie moved to Gina's side. "What do you need?"

Gina pulled out her journal, glad she'd included some of the notes about purification rituals just in case. "Each step of the ritual would have included a bowl of water. We just need to leave enough weight on the ledges to match that."

"Each one?" Will asked, looking down the length of the tunnel.

"No." Gina paused, skimming the notes but already knowing she was reaching a dangerous point. Her eyes found the passage in question.

"So how many of them do we gotta put stuff on?" Owen asked. He'd already dug a handful of protein bars from his pack. He gave a half-grin as he waved them. "I'll be happy to never see another one of these in my life. We'll use them to get that pressure you need."

How many was the question indeed. She read over the notes twice more. "Um…"

"What's wrong?" Dieter asked, keeping his voice quiet as he moved to read over her shoulder.

She wasn't entirely sure how to explain her hesitancy. Kaufman had translated the inscription ages before she'd even studied the language and had determined there were six steps to the ritual. Based on his findings, they'd need to put weights on the first six ledges.

But that was the problem. She'd gone back over his work herself about a year back, after she'd gained more confidence in her skills with the language. And she'd found seven steps. If she was right, they needed weights on the first seven ledges.

She pushed the translation toward Dieter. "How many steps did you find in the rituals?"

"I haven't studied those in some time." He skimmed the page. "Six, aren't there?"

He was probably right. She'd always wondered if she'd made a mistake, misunderstood something. For all of Kaufman's arrogance, and even though he'd missed the 'soar' translation, he was still the reigning authority on the Mevoyan language. He'd picked apart these writings for years. She'd only gone over the rituals once or twice. She'd be a fool to assume herself a better authority on the subject than him.

"Right," she said. "Six." She took the bars from Owen and gauged them in her hands, then carefully stacked seven of them on the first counter-height ledge. It sank an inch. She'd expected the movement, but it still sent a jolt through her heart. If she was wrong…

Nothing happened. No rumbles. No creatures. Nothing.

She exhaled and moved on to the next one. The rest of the protein bars in her hands went on that. It, too, dipped an inch, and nothing further happened.

"Looks like they got it right." Lettie gave Burke a smug look.

He rolled his eyes.

"We need more things to weigh these down," Gina said, taking off her pack to see what they had on hand.

"Take Burke's sleeping bag," Lich said. "He's not sleeping anyway."

He glared at her. "Volunteer your own crap."

"Sure, take mine." She tossed her sleeping bag at Gina. Dieter caught it before it hit her in the head. Lich winked at Shrimpy. "I'm sure I'll find someone to share with."

Shrimply almost looked embarrassed.

Dieter set the bag on the next ledge.

"Here," Shrimpy said, holding out a bottle of water.

"Not that," Will said. "We lost a lot of the gear back when…" He paused with a glance at Gina. "I mean, clean water's the most important thing we've got, and we don't have a whole lot left. We need to conserve it."

Gina exhaled and hoped once again that the purification ritual was a sign they were close to the ruby and the exit.

"Well, how about this?" Shrimpy offered his rock axe instead. "There hasn't been much need for these, and we still have yours and Owen's."

Will nodded his assent. The fourth ledge dipped an inch.

The camera case with a couple of candy bars surrendered from Owen was enough to tip ledge five, and ledge six held a romance novel Lich surrendered and a few makeup items from Lettie's bag. As soon as ledge six sank, a faint rumbling sound came from deep within the walls.

Gina froze, waiting for something to crash down on them, but the rumblings stopped. Nothing happened.

"That's it," Dieter said. "It should be safe for us to continue now."

Gina's eyes fixed on the seventh ledge, but she tore her gaze away. The rumbling sound had only confirmed her suspicions. Kaufman had gotten it right. She'd been mistaken.

Will nodded and led them onward. They were already far enough down the tunnel to faintly make out the other end by the light of their LEDs. It seemed to open into a larger space, but the headlamps and lanterns couldn't quite reach the other end of the space to show its dimensions.

Gina kept her eyes open for any signs of further directions, but the walls remained bare as they passed the eighth ledge. Then the ninth. She sighed. It looked like they were clear.

The cave rumbled. The ceiling split with a loud crack.

"Cave-in!" Will shouted. "Run!"

Gina staggered for balance as the ground shook beneath her feet. Dieter caught her arm and propelled her forward. Lettie shrieked and stumbled, and he turned his attention to helping her instead.

The ground shook harder, and pebbles began cascading down from the ceiling, then softball-sized rocks. Gina found her feet and managed to clumsily move onward. Burke passed her easily, then Owen.

"Come on, run!" Will shouted again.

Gina struggled to focus. To run. Her legs churned almost uselessly against the shaking ground. Was she moving forward at all? Panic filled her throat, choking her.

A rock hit her shoulder, and she fell against the wall, flickering lights of pain dotting her vision. A massive rock crashed to the ground just in front of her.

She had to move. Had to get out of the tunnel before she was trapped.

The thought inspired a terror that gave her a new burst of adrenaline. She pushed herself upright, staggered around the boulder, and forced herself forward. Another rock grazed her arm, and she fought to ignore the pain and continue on. Someone was shouting, but the thunder of the cascading rocks drowned them out.

A rock hit the side of her head. Everything vanished into a pit of blackness.

★ ★ ★

Gina opened her eyes to find blackness equal to the pit that had swallowed her before. She'd done something wrong. Her eyes were still closed. She tried opening them again, but her brain informed her that they were already open. Her hand lifted, ready to search out her face and confirm that her eyes must be, in fact, closed, but pain tore through her arm at the movement, drawing a groan.

"Stay still," Dieter's voice whispered. "You're safe."

She turned toward his voice, but still saw nothing but black. "Dieter?" Panic edged her tone. "I can't open my eyes. I can't see anything."

"It's okay. You're safe."

Her other arm cooperated with less pain. She reached for her eyes and found them open. "I'm blind." With fumbling fingers, she sought him out. "I'm blind!"

"Shield your eyes."

"What? I can't—"

"Shield them." His voice held that same calm authority as before.

She found her eyes again and covered them. "Okay."

A light flared between her fingertips. She blinked a couple of times at the brightness, then lifted her hand.

The first thing she saw was a long slab of solid rock jutting from a smoothed rock wall to her left. The tunnel wall. She lay underneath one of the ledges.

Dieter lay beside her, holding a lighter, yellow flame burning low. Behind him, rocks of varying sizes formed another wall. She tilted her head and winced at the immediate pain shooting through her skull. She squinted despite the pain and managed to see the same piles of rocks above and below.

The light flicked out.

Her fear spiked again. "Please turn it back on."

His tone of voice didn't change. "We're within a couple of yards from the end of the tunnel. It shouldn't take the others long to dig us out."

"But we can still have light, right?" The white glow in her vision from where the light had burned still danced in the blackness.

"It shouldn't take long. But I'm not sure exactly how long."

She didn't get it. His tone hinted that there was something he was trying to avoid saying out loud, something he didn't want to address. Her pain-dulled brain wasn't quite connecting whatever it was. They weren't far from the end, he'd said. The others were digging them out.

Her eyes widened. They were still in the tunnel. They'd been caught in the collapse.

They were buried alive.

# Chapter 10

Gina gasped. Her chest constricted, and her throat tightened. Her good hand pushed upward, to the side, anywhere, searching for something that would give and open to freedom. She couldn't breathe. Had to get out.

Dieter's hand clamped on her wrist and pushed her arm back down. "Stay calm."

Calm? Was he kidding? "Let go! We have to get out!"

His other hand slid over her forehead. He pressed his fingertips into her temples. His breath felt hot against her ear. "You need to calm down. Be still. They will find us. You are not helping yourself or us by panicking."

She struggled, fighting against him, against the pounding in her head, against the nausea rising through her system.

"Now breathe in slowly. Let it out. Slowly in…"

The pressure against her temple began to override the sensations of terror through her body. His quiet, calm voice broke through the panic. As he continued speaking softly into her ear, she gradually began to draw air in and let it out, following his coaching. Her chest and throat relaxed, letting her breathe steadily once more.

After a minute, he gently released her arm and temples.

She closed her eyes and remained still, focusing on her breathing. It would be okay. He said they were near the end. The others would rescue them.

Unless the others had also gotten caught in the cave-in. Or unless the others thought she and Dieter had been killed and didn't come looking at all.

She clenched her teeth and forced her attention back to her breathing. She couldn't think like that, or she'd panic again. Use up all their air before they had a chance to be rescued.

The silence stretched on until it became oppressive. She opened her eyes, though she still couldn't see in the blackness. "Was this a mistake?"

"What?"

"Coming here. All the people who've died in this cave, and now we're stuck in here, and if we don't make it out, the others won't have anyone to guide them, and they'll get killed by traps, and—"

"Everyone knew the risks. They chose to come with us."

"You were ahead of me. You should've stayed clear of the tunnel. Then at least they'd have one person to help guide them."

"Don't be silly. I can't translate clearly without you any more than you can translate clearly without me."

Translations flicked through her mind. She exhaled. "This was my fault."

"Don't blame yourself. I'm not certain what triggered the trap, but it didn't relate to the purification ritual. It was something else. I missed it, too, whatever it might have been."

"No." Tears wanted to come, but the regrets weighed too heavily on her to allow for even that. She just felt numb. And stupid. "It was seven. I mean, there are seven steps to the ritual. Kaufman got the interpretation wrong. I knew it, but I thought was the one who'd gotten it wrong, so I didn't say anything."

He didn't speak for a moment. "So we should have placed weight on the seventh ledge."

The tears did leak now. "I could've gotten everyone killed. This was a mistake, coming down here at all. I never should have—"

His hand found hers and squeezed. "It wasn't a mistake. We're going to find the ruby. Everyone who was lost will be remembered as heroes. Now quiet down. Don't waste the air."

She fell silent but didn't let go of his hand. He didn't let go, either.

As hard as it had been to gauge the passage of time before, it was impossible here. Nothing to see but interminable blackness. Nothing to hear but her own and Dieter's breathing. She almost spoke up more than once, wondering why it was taking the searchers so long, but she realized that it might have only been a few minutes. Or an hour. It was impossible to tell.

This must be what it's like to be a dog.

She almost laughed out loud at the thought. She was getting hysterical. Closing her eyes again, she forced herself to focus on her breathing once more. Inhale. Exhale. Repeat.

The rock under her wasn't as cold as it had been. In fact, the whole space was starting to feel warm. Stuffy.

Something in her mind whispered that this meant they were running out of air, but she had a hard time convincing herself that she should care. She just felt heavy. Sleepy.

"We're going to die," she whispered, her voice hoarse.

"They'll find us." His voice sounded as drowsy and weak as her own.

She squeezed his hand again. "It's been an honor working with you."

"Don't talk like that."

"Really, I mean it. Other people thought I was silly for pursuing this field. You were the first person to take me seriously and want to work with me." She shifted her weight and managed to rest her head against his shoulder. "Thank you. It truly has been an honor."

He didn't answer for a moment. When he spoke, his voice was even quieter than before. "The honor has been all mine."

Gina closed her eyes again, unsure when exactly she'd opened them. It was hard to tell, with no difference to tell her when they were open. Not that it really mattered anymore.

A touch of cold air made her shiver. It figured that the universe would force one last discomfort on her before death.

The cold sensation grew. Her foggy brain took a moment before clicking.

Cold air meant fresh air.

Her eyes flew open. Cracks of light had appeared between the rocks on the other side of Dieter.

"Dieter," she whispered, shaking him.

"Mm?" was the groggy response.

"Dieter, the light…"

The cool air continued coming in, and she filled her lungs with it. The heavy, tired feelings melted away into new energy.

"Hey," she called as loudly as she could. "Hey, we're in here!"

Dieter blinked in the growing light. "We're here," he called.

Muffled voices responded.

Dieter flashed her a grin. "Told you they'd find us."

It wasn't long before the rocks beside them shifted. Hands lifted a few aside, and Will blinked in at them. "We've got them!"

More rocks moved aside. Will and Owen reached in and helped Dieter squeeze out of the space.

As soon as they vanished, Savion appeared in the opening and lifted Gina out like she was a doll. He set her on her feet but kept one arm wrapped around her, helping her over the uneven rocks until they were clear of the tunnel.

Her brain told her that she should be feeling some sense of fear and intimidation right about now, but the relief was too strong to allow for such feelings. She clung to him instead, hugging him in gratitude. He stiffened slightly, but gently patted her back before disentangling her and helping her sit on a larger rock near the tunnel's exit.

"We thought we'd lost you guys," Owen said.

Burke shone a light in Gina's eyes. "What hurts?"

"I was so scared," Lettie wailed, dropping to Gina's side.

"My head, mostly, and my arm," Gina said.

"I thought you'd gone nuts when you ran back in," Will told Dieter. "Didn't see she'd fallen back there."

"Wiggle your fingers," Burke said, continuing his exam.

Lettie sniffled. "And then all the rocks stopped moving, and you guys were gone!"

"You must have some sort of crazy luck in you." Owen looked back at the tunnel, a distant look on his face.

"I thought you were dead," Lettie wailed, clutching Gina.

"You'll be fine, just bruised and sore." Burke turned to Dieter.

Gina looked around, noting a conspicuous absence. Shrimpy and Lich weren't there. She opened her mouth to ask after them but closed it. She couldn't very well ask about them when she wasn't even sure she had their names right, could she?

"Where are Sheila and Paul?" Dieter asked.

Gina glanced at him, surprised. Apparently, he had a better memory for names than she did.

Owen kept his back to them, still staring at the tunnel. "They weren't as lucky as you. Didn't make it under one of those ledges."

"They're still in there?" Dieter stood, turning to the tunnel.

Owen shook his head. "We found them."

No one spoke for a moment. Lettie sniffled and clung to Gina. Gina, for her part, couldn't manage to lift her gaze from the floor. She'd barely noticed the two extra packs on the floor near Owen's feet, but now they were all she could think of. Two packs. Two more people lost. Two more that she'd failed.

"I'm sorry," Dieter said quietly.

Owen's head bobbed, then he turned his back on the tunnel. "We better carry on."

Will gave Gina a hesitant glance. "Should we rest a minute?"

Gina looked around. The space they were in was relatively small, compared to the other rooms that followed traps. Almost as if the cave knew their numbers had thinned. She shuddered and pushed the thought away, feeling dirty for even thinking it. The ceiling sat only inches above Savion's head, and the walls were rounded into an oval sort of space before continuing on in another one of the winding tunnels she'd gotten so used to.

Owen was right. They should keep going. Finding the ruby was the only way to make things right, to make the sacrifices mean anything. She stood and hoped with everything in her that the legends were right, that the Spanish ship had crashed at least close to the pool. If it hadn't...

She stood, turning her back on those thoughts physically as well as mentally. "Let's go."

The group remained quiet for the first half hour of walking. Then Lettie finished sniffling and slid to Gina's side. "You said this means we're close, right? We'll find it soon?"

"I think so. Ritual purity was a temporary state to the Mevoyan people. If the tunnel really was designed for the purity ceremony, then the pool shouldn't be far after that. Otherwise, whoever went through the ritual would have to do it all over again before they reached the ruby."

"Will there be more traps?"

"Some, but not as active as the ones we've found so far." She thought for a moment. "It said something about toxic water, which we're pretty sure is either near the pool or in the pool itself, so we need to be careful not to touch any water we find in that area."

"Everyone hear that?" Lettie asked loudly. "No one touch any water. Except the stuff we brought with us, I mean."

"I think that's all we know about at this point. There may be more instructions in the cavern with the pool when we get there."

"But you aren't even sure it'll be in that pool, right?" Burke said. "The Spaniards took it out of there."

"The legend says the ship was returned to the original resting place of the ruby. We know that this cave system is close to the ocean, and based on the writings, the exit should open onto a beach of some sort. It's possible that whatever hurricane destroyed the ship could have carried it back into the cave system. It might not be exactly in the pool, but it should be close."

He shrugged.

The lights flashed on something shiny. Gina glanced up and saw the tunnel narrowing ahead with glossy stones set in either side of the narrower point. A similarly glossy stone with carved writing stood above the entryway.

"Stop for a second," she said, tapping Will's shoulder. "We better check that translation before we go any further." She pulled out her journal and started copying down the words, glancing to her side for Dieter's analysis.

Dieter wasn't there.

She turned. "Dieter?"

No answer. The others glanced back with her, but Dieter was no longer with the group.

Neither was Owen.

A pang of fear shot through Gina's chest. Something had happened. Images of Ondiers floated before her eyes once more. Owen was the Ondier, and now he was killing again. "Dieter!" she gasped and darted back the way they'd come, nearly dropping her journal in her panic. Voices and footsteps clattered behind her as the others raced after her.

She neared a corner, heart pounding. It had to be a mistake. There was no Ondier. The men had just stopped to relieve themselves.

Or there was an Ondier, and it was going to kill them all.

She raised her journal like a weapon and rounded the corner.

Dieter looked up, startled. Blood coated his hands and mouth.

Owen lay at his feet, eyes fixed on the ceiling. His skin hung in tatters from the bones.

Just like Jake.

Bile burned Gina's throat as her brain descended into a blur of confusion. No. This couldn't be right. There had to be some mistake. Dieter couldn't be…

Gasps and cries joined the blur around her as the others rounded the corner. Lettie staggered into the wall and clung to it, her mouth moving through words that wouldn't come.

Dieter's eyes flicked over the group, then his face calmed. He straightened. His lips turned upward into what was almost a smile. "Well. This is awkward."

Burke was the first to recover. He yanked his pack free and raised it to strike. "You son of a—"

"Kill me if you wish." Dieter picked up a shred of Owen's shirt and primly wiped his mouth. "So long as you're certain you can safely navigate the remainder of the cave system without my translation skills."

Burke slowed. Looked back at Gina.

She still couldn't think straight. This was impossible. She'd worked with Dieter for years. How could he be an Ondier?

Dieter licked his fingertips clean, then finished removing the blood from his hands with the rag. "Foolish of me to act so quickly in eliminating Owen. I'm afraid I hadn't much choice in the matter, though. He'd nearly figured out who I am. I couldn't have him whispering his suspicions to the rest of you." He chuckled drily and dropped the red-stained cloth. "Not that it matters now. Pity."

Savion stepped forward, his eyes burning. "You will die for what you have done, monster."

"I already stated the conditions. If you feel they are met, feel free to carry on with your murderous intents."

Will put out a hand, stopping Savion before he could continue. The smaller man looked back at Gina. "You can do it, right? You can translate without his help?" His eyes pleaded for her to say yes.

Her voice came out a whisper. "No."

Lettie threw up. She turned away, sobbing.

"Of course you can," Burke snapped. "You let him get in your head, thinking you aren't capable, but you're better than him. You'll do just fine without him."

Her legs wouldn't hold her up anymore. She fumbled her way to the side of the tunnel and sagged against it. Her eyes, against her will, found Dieter's face. His smile broadened. He knew the truth. She knew it, too, and it made her sick.

She tore her gaze away. "I can't. I'm only good at the technical meanings of the words, their definitions. He's the one who figures out the context and what they actually mean."

"But that's what 'definition' means," Burke pressed, 'duh' in his tone.

She shook her head. "'Cave of sky on butter mountain, milk flow down over rest.'"

Will stared at her, uncomprehending. Even Burke and Savion shot puzzled frowns her way.

"What the heck's that supposed to mean?" Burke demanded.

"Exactly. That's what I came up with when I translated a passage just a month ago. I know 'butter mountain' refers to the nearby mountain range, but the rest was lost to me." She exhaled, hating herself for the next words she had to say. "Dieter had to finish the translation. 'When the sky is dark over those mountains, it'll rain before nightfall.' I can figure out what the words translate to in English, but I can't figure out the nuances of the meanings."

Burke's expression soured. He knew what she was about to say next.

She forced herself to say it out loud anyway. "I can't translate without him. He can't translate without me. If we're going to get out of this cave in one piece, it's going to take both of us."

That's why he went back for her in the tunnel, she realized. He'd saved her from the cave-in not because he cared about her, but because he knew he couldn't translate without her. She felt sick again.

The others remained silent, internal wars playing out on their faces. Savion finally stepped back.

Burke kept his pack at the ready. "How do we know he'll translate correctly now? He'll lead us into a trap and kill us all."

Dieter snorted.

Gina looked up at him, startled. His eyes glimmered, as if waiting for her to come to a conclusion she should have already made.

It took only a moment for her mind to make the connection. "He wants the ruby." Her voice came out flat. "And he needs our help to find it. He won't kill us off as long as he thinks we're of use."

Burke's eyes narrowed. "What's he want the ruby for?"

Gina shrugged.

"It's worth a lot of money," Will said quietly. "Money can go far to help a monster stay hidden."

Gina chanced another look at Dieter. His expression had settled into a vaguely smug look. Will was right. Dieter didn't care about the Mevoyan culture or heritage. He didn't care about her. He was just in it for the money.

"And what about after we find the ruby?" Burke asked.

Gina didn't have an answer to that.

The smug look on Dieter's face morphed into a smirk.

A flash of anger shot through her, tearing aside the last traces of shock. How dare he? The workers who had gone missing. Jake. Owen. All those murders, all that time pretending to be on their side, pretending to be her friend…

She stood up, fury giving her new energy. "But none of that means we have to trust him. Tie him up. Savion, keep your eyes on him at all times. Don't let him so much as twitch out of line."

Dieter's smirk broadened. "I always wondered what it might take for you to find a backbone."

She seethed but held it inside. He thought he was just biding his time and would kill them once he no longer needed them. She felt the same about him. As soon as they made it out of these wretched caves, she'd see to it that he received justice for all he'd done.

Savion bound Dieter's hands in front of him with a bit more roughness than the task actually demanded. It would have helped Gina feel somewhat better, but Dieter's maddeningly calm and unchanging expression ruined it. She turned away, ignoring the sour taste in her mouth.

Lettie gripped her arm. "What about…" Her eyes flickered back toward Owen's body.

Gina felt sick again.

"The collapsed tunnel," Savion said quietly. "We will place him with his friends."

Burke grunted in displeasure. "Hurry up."

Gina turned away from it all as Savion and Will dealt with the body, leaving Burke to guard Dieter. This couldn't be happening. It just couldn't. She felt his eyes fixed on her and wanted to throw up.

By the time Savion and Will returned, she was ready to be done with the entire expedition. If the way had been clear, she would've run full speed back to the ravine, climbed out whether she had a harness or not, and kept running all the way back to the States. She didn't care about the ruby or the Mevoyan culture or even the others around her anymore. She wanted to wake up in bed and discover this had all just been a bad dream.

Lettie's sniffles forced Gina back to reality. There was no way back. Only forward. She did her best to pull herself together. "Let's go."

Her heart dipped low as they returned to the narrow area. That's why she'd gone to find Dieter in the first place. She needed help with a translation.

She looked over her shoulder. Savion and Burke guarded Dieter on either side, but he ignored them. His eyes were set on her.

Gina couldn't bring herself to speak to him yet. She turned away. Maybe she could do this herself. The journal was still in her hands. She'd forgotten all about it in the fuss. Opening it to the page with the copied translation she'd made, she double-checked the symbols against her transcription, then set to work.

"Well?" Burke's voice was sharp with impatience.

She exhaled. "Uh…" All she'd gotten so far was the name of the ruby. The rest was a jumble of nonsense. Something about a bird and the sky and the ocean.

"She requires his help," Savion said.

Acid burned at the back of her throat. She didn't want his help. She didn't want to look at him.

But Savion was right. She needed Dieter.

She turned to find him standing right behind her. Her heart leapt in a frantic staccato.

His smirk never wavered. "Did I startle you?"

"Hardly." She somehow managed to keep her voice from squeaking too much as she spoke.

He waited.

Gina took a deep breath, forcing herself to calm down. Savion and Burke stood close, watching. They'd keep him from trying anything. Besides, as much as she needed him, he needed her. She was safe.

For now.

Pushing the thoughts aside, she turned the journal to face him. "This. I can't get this part."

He continued watching her for a moment, then shifted his gaze to the page. His eyes flicked across the symbols, then her translation. The smirk gradually faded as he became lost in his study. "A great, winged beast," he said, "drew out of the sky—"

Forgetting herself, she pointed to the words. "Not 'drew.' I think it should be 'appeared.'"

He glanced at her.

She quickly withdrew her hand.

"Right." He returned to the words. "Appeared out of the sky, bearing…" He looked up at the symbols again. "The Ruby of Ages. It's their story of how they found the gem."

"Really?" She focused on the page. Other writings had contained hints about the Mevoyan legend of how they'd received the ruby, but no one had ever found a complete copy of the story.

"It's all here." Excitement picked up in his voice. "The great winged beast gifted them with the ruby and showed—no, promised—that it would bring them great power if they used it correctly. Look," he pointed to a symbol, "that means 'fool,' right?"

"A foolish person or foolish action, depending on context. Or it could mean llama."

He shook his head. "It's 'foolish person' here. A foolish person tried to use the ruby's power, and it tore the sky asunder and caused the seas to rise up against them. They…" He pointed to a word.

She squinted. "End?"

He nodded, taking another moment to study the words before continuing. "They had to kill the fool in order to satisfy the ruby's power, and the sky and oceans calmed. They realized that this gem truly was powerful, but they must never use that power except in times of great need." He looked up at her. The thrill of discovery made his eyes gleam. "We found it."

"The whole legend," she breathed. She smiled, but her smile froze. No. This wasn't the same Dieter she'd spent countless hours researching and studying alongside. This was a monster. No matter how much he acted like her old friend.

She snapped the journal shut. "It's a valuable discovery," she told the others, "but it doesn't look like there are any traps here. We're safe to continue." She took a deep breath, trying to steady herself and ignore Dieter's watchful gaze. "Get pictures of that carving, then we need to continue on."

Lettie was still shaking too hard to photograph the legend, so Gina took the camera from her and did it herself. The faster they could move on, the sooner they could be done. And rid of Dieter.

Will once again took the lead. Gina and Lettie followed. Savion and Burke walked Dieter behind them. Lettie glanced backwards every few steps, anxiety on her face. Gina sighed. She'd rather not have him walking behind her, but she needed to stay near the front where she could see. She didn't think she'd feel any better or safer if she was behind him, anyway. The best she could do was to keep her gaze forward and pretend he wasn't there.

A clicking sound rattled down the tunnel. A metal grate dropped from the ceiling in front of them, closing off the way forward. Before they could react, a second one dropped behind them.

Will stepped forward, grabbed the bars on the first grate, and pulled upwards. It didn't budge. Savion turned to the ones behind them and tried the same thing with equal results.

They were trapped.

# Chapter 11

Lettie shrieked.

Gina spun on Dieter. "What good did that do, hiding the part about the trap? Now you're stuck, too!"

His eyes narrowed at the first grate, then the second. She had to be imagining it, but he almost looked puzzled.

Burke shoved him, malice in his eyes. "Thought you'd walk us into a trap, huh?"

"Look at it," Dieter said. His gaze had returned to Gina.

She'd missed something. She turned and frowned at the grate before them.

"I told you, we should just kill him and be done with it," Burke pressed. "If he isn't going to bother to translate it right, then what's the point of keeping him around?"

Metal bars crossed with each other, thick and rusty. Iron. No, steel. Spikes pointed out from most of the places where the bars crossed. They looked similar to the Mevoyan lances, but only had two edges instead of four. The edges and pointed ends still looked plenty sharp, though. It appeared that some had rusted away or fallen off with time. The grate rested along the outside of the stone tunnel along the bottom and sides. The top…

She frowned. Were those bolts? And gears? The gears rested on metal tracks that ran between the two grates, most likely how they'd dropped from the ceiling. No one had been looking upward, or they would have seen the trap before they'd walked into it.

"Perhaps that would be best," Will said.

Dieter's eyes remained fixed on Gina.

She shook her head. "This isn't a Mevoyan trap."

"What are you talking about?" Burke demanded. "This whole place was built by them. How could this trap not be one of theirs?"

"It's anachronistic," she said.

His frown didn't change, though a slightly blank look appeared in his eyes.

"The metal used, the gears and bolts—the Mevoyan people didn't have that sort of technology." She touched the grate and looked up at the mechanisms at the top. "But the Spanish did, six centuries ago."

"When the Spaniards found the ruby," Lettie said. Her voice only shook a little. She seemed to be recovering.

Gina nodded and hazarded a glance at Dieter. He looked satisfied.

"Why would the Spaniards go to all this trouble?" Will asked.

"I'm not sure." Gina studied the mechanisms again. "Maybe they thought someone was following them. Or they thought they'd need to return sometime and wanted to make sure no one else passed through the cave before they returned. Regardless, this was their trap. Anyone know anything about fifteenth-century Spanish traps?"

Blank looks all around.

"Right." She sighed and held her lantern higher to get a better view. "Does that look like a switch to you?"

Will peered at the spot she pointed to, his headlamp adding more light. "Kind of."

"But what will it do?" Burke asked. "You're just going to flip a switch and hope for the best? Because that strategy's been working great for us so far."

"This trap was from the Spaniards, not the Mevoyan people," Savion said.

"He's right," Gina said. "It's different. They would've built in a failsafe, some way to make sure they could get out if they got caught in their own trap."

"Are there any other switches or levers?" Will asked.

Good question, Gina realized. She shouldn't have stopped looking just because she'd found one possible switch. They all shone their lights upward, scanning the length of the tracks and studying the mechanisms.

"There's something," Savion said. His light shone outward, into the tunnel behind them.

Gina squinted at the spot and saw a small metal lever sticking out of the ceiling a few feet back.

"Great. How are we supposed to reach that?" Burke asked.

"It's probably how they would have kept the trap from falling on them as they walked through," Gina said.

"And how does that help?" Burke pressed.

Gina turned back to the first switch. "It doesn't mean this isn't still some sort of failsafe."

Will reached up toward the switch. Even with his lanky height, he could barely reach. He paused and glanced around at the others. "We're trying it?"

"I don't think we should," Burke grunted.

"It's the best option we have," Dieter said.

Burke shoved him. "No one asked you."

Dieter shrugged, unconcerned.

"He's right, though," Lettie said. "We can't reach the one back there."

"So it's this, or sit around and wait for Spaniards to show up and let us out," Dieter supplied.

Burke shoved him again.

Will cast a questioning look at Savion.

The large man nodded.

Will flipped the switch.

The gears ground for a moment, then began to turn.

The grate in front of them lurched and began to move. Toward them.

Gina took a step back. It had to turn at some point, right? To return to its place on the ceiling and let them free?

It didn't.

Lettie stumbled backwards, eyes wide. "It's closing on us!"

The blades sticking inward took on an entirely new meaning. Gina stepped back, eyes frantically searching for a way out. There had to be a failsafe somewhere inside the trap. Didn't there?

"A moving, spiked wall?" Burke asked. The skepticism in his tone was mixed with fear. "Isn't that cliché?"

"You can tell the Spaniards that," Gina said, still searching. "There has to be another switch."

Dieter stepped forward. Savion caught his shoulder and pulled him back.

Dieter glared at the man, then turned to Gina. "Fifteenth century gears."

She blinked. Right. She searched the floor for a loose rock. Finding none, she dug into her pack and yanked out the first solid object her hand hit, the small first-aid kit. She shoved it into Savion's hands. "Push that into the gears."

He stared at her.

She pointed to the gear grinding along the track. "There! Push it there!"

Understanding seemed to dawn. He stepped forward and crammed the edge of the kit against the gear. It rolled forward a little further, then slowed, groaning against the solid plastic blocking its progress.

Lettie sighed in relief. "You did it."

The kit cracked, then buckled. The gear resumed its path forward.

Burke pulled out a rock axe. "Try this."

Savion took it and wedged it into the gear. It slowed, but the edge of the axe skipped over the lower teeth, allowing the grate to edge closer.

"Angle it," Burke demanded, the fear in his voice beginning to take over.

"Hurry," Gina pleaded.

Savion gripped the axe handle with both hands and tilted and wedged until it caught. The gear whined and finally came to a stop.

Gina melted against the tunnel wall and took a few deep breaths before looking around again. The two grates were only about four feet away from each other now. Barely enough room for the five of them to fit between.

"Will, can you reach the other switch?" she asked. Of all of them, his skinny, long arms were the most likely to cover the gap.

"I can try." He carefully weaved his body between the blades on the rear wall to press as close to the grate as possible, then stretched his arm through one of the holes. His fingers fell short by at least a foot.

The gears slipped another notch forward, drawing a squeak from Lettie and a grunt of surprise from Burke.

Gina made no noise, but her heart jumped back into double time. "We have to get the other lever. How can we reach it?"

They all looked around, helpless for anything that might help.

"A ruler," Lettie burst out.

Burke gave her a look. "Sure, I packed that right next to my protractor."

"No, I mean..." She shook her head.

Gina recognized the frustrated look on her friend's face. When Lettie was overly excited about anything, it sometimes took her longer to get her thoughts into words. "Take a breath, Lettie."

The petite woman sucked in a breath. "When I'm at home and something falls under the couch, I get a ruler and use it to swipe it back out."

Will's eyes lit up. "Help me reach my axe."

Burke looked dubious, but he worked his hand around the spikes and helped Will free the rock axe strapped to the wiry man's belt.

The gears lurched forward another notch. Savion readjusted his axe, trying to brace it.

Will stretched his free arm out once more, the long tool in hand this time. It scraped against the tunnel wall as he awkwardly maneuvered it upwards.

The gears slipped another notch and broke free. Gina gasped and lunged forward, grabbing the bars of the grate and pushing with her legs, but her feet only skidded along the cobblestone floor. Lettie screamed. Burke joined Gina, but the grate continued pushing forward. Something sharp hit Gina's ankle. She glanced back to see the other grate. Too close.

Savion managed to get the axe wedged in place again. The grate ground to a halt. Only two feet to spare.

"Hurry!" Lettie cried, clutching at Will.

Burke quickly pulled her off him before she ruined his focus.

Will's face twisted in concentration. He pushed and pulled at the axe, but it kept sliding just inches too low. "It's not long enough. It's not working."

The grate shuddered as the gear slipped again. Savion held the axe firm.

"Do we have anything longer?" Gina asked, searching the space with her eyes. She saw nothing else they could use.

"You can reach," Dieter said quietly.

The gear slid another couple of notches.

Will winced and pushed harder, turning his head away and twisting his shoulders to push as much of himself through the small hole as physically possible. He blindly scraped the axe against the wall behind him.

"Higher," Gina coached. "More… more… Now forward."

It missed.

"You almost got it. Higher again. No, more. Now pull!"

The edge of the axe head caught against the lever but skipped off it instead of pulling it.

The gear slipped again.

Lettie whimpered.

"He can't get it," Burke said.

"He can," Gina insisted. "One more try, Will. You can do this." She coached him again until the axe was in position. "Pull!"

It caught the lever. Flipped it.

The gears groaned. Then the grate moved again, this time away from them.

Gina almost collapsed in relief again. "You did it. You got it."

The grate clanged against the other end of the track, then began swinging in and up to open the way through.

Lettie and Will both cheered.

Burke looked like he might cheer, then caught himself. "Finally."

Even Savion cracked a smile.

Gina straightened. "Okay. Let's keep moving."

The gears groaned again. Will yelped as the grate he was tangled in began to rise, carrying him with it.

"Hey!" Gina grabbed at the edge of the grate. Savion's hands landed beside hers, but the grate continued to rise. She glanced upward. There wasn't enough clearance on the ceiling. Will would be crushed. "Come on, help!"

Lettie grabbed hold and pulled downward, but it didn't make a difference. Burke turned back and pulled as well. Gina sagged back against her arms, putting her full weight into the task. Lettie did the same. The grate slowed, but still pressed onward.

Dieter silently ducked between their legs and under the grate, straightening neatly on the other side.

A pang of fear shot through Gina. "What are you doing?" He was going to reactivate the trap. Kill them all.

He jumped on the other side of the grate, climbing a few spaces up until he could reach the mechanism at the top through the higher holes. He slid his bound hands through, grabbed one of the bolts on the gear, and yanked.

The bolt shuddered and popped free. The gear whined only a moment before the mechanism crumbled in on itself. The grate dropped free with a clang, sending Gina and the others tumbling to the floor.

Will extricated himself as quickly as possible without the spikes slicing him open, then staggered a few steps away from the grate. He leaned against the wall, puffing for air.

Dieter tossed the bolt aside and climbed back down, his movements smooth and calm. He lifted the grate, which now swung loose, and walked back under it to rejoin them.

Lettie stared at him, her eyes wide and slightly puzzled. "You saved his life."

He turned his gaze forward. "Are we continuing?"

Savion stood and returned to his post at Dieter's side. Burke quickly followed suit, though he was still panting.

Will looked at Dieter like he couldn't quite believe what had just happened. "I… thanks."

Dieter simply nodded.

Gina still couldn't believe it herself. But part of her wasn't surprised in the least. That part whispered that Dieter hadn't actually changed from the person she'd known all these years. He was still the same Dieter. And the Dieter she knew wouldn't hesitate to save someone.

She looked up at the destroyed mechanics above them. Her eyes drifted to the other side of the machine, the grate that was already tucked back into place against the ceiling.

She frowned. "Why didn't you do that with the other one in the first place?"

His eyes flicked in her direction. "The other mechanism is more complex. It would have taken too long to disable it."

"Besides, Will was able to reach the lever," Lettie supplied. Her eyes shone a little. "Like Dieter said."

Something still felt off to Gina, and Lettie's gushing wasn't helping matters. "Let's keep moving."

Gina remained on alert as they continued on, now watching for Spanish traps as well. And for signs of trouble from behind her. She peeked over her shoulder. The path wasn't quite wide enough for the men to all walk side by side anymore. Burke walked beside Dieter, occasionally giving him a shove forward. Savion hovered behind the two, his eyes flicking from Dieter to their surroundings and back again.

Too many dangers. Too many things to watch. She exhaled and turned back forward. They'd make it through this somehow. They had to.

Over an hour passed in silence, the familiar quiet trudge through the lengthy, twisting tunnels. The monotony of the hike lulled Gina to the point that she almost didn't notice when Will stopped. Startled, she looked up, then checked behind herself, a nagging fear at the back of her mind. But Dieter hadn't stepped out of line. He looked almost docile, his hands bound and that same calm expression on his face.

"What's up?" Gina asked, returning her attention to Will.

He pointed his light at the wall. "More writing."

The hallway narrowed further just ahead. They'd have to walk single-file to get through. Perfect place for a trap, either from the Mevoyan people or from the

Spaniards. She aimed her light at the ceiling but saw no signs of steel tracks or grates. Maybe the previous trap was the only one the Spaniards had left.

She turned back to the writing Will had found and pulled out her journal. She felt a presence beside her. Dieter. Her heart only jolted a little. Of course he'd approached. He had to help translate. Still, her legs shifted a couple steps away without conscious command.

"Here," Lettie said, holding out a hand. "I'll take the pictures."

Gina handed over the camera, glad for an excuse to take another small step away from Dieter. "Thanks." While Lettie's flashes added more shadows and light to the tunnel, Gina set to work copying and translating the symbols in the notebook.

"That one," Dieter said, tapping one of the words, his movement made awkward by his bound hands. "I don't think that's 'clean.'"

He'd gotten beside her again. Rats. She exhaled and looked at her translation. "What do you think it is?"

"I'll have to see the rest of the context."

Shaking her head, she resumed her work. It took a few minutes and two consultations with her notes from the other notebook, but finally she had her rough translation down.

Dieter leaned over her shoulder, eyes on the journal.

Too close. She ducked a half-step away and held the journal out where he could still comfortably see it.

His eyes glittered on her for a moment, then returned to the page. "'Pure.' This first part is referring to the purification ritual. 'Those who have been purified and deemed worthy to approach the gem…'" He paused and tapped another word. "Are you sure that's 'child'?"

She returned to the notebook, leafing through to find the needed reference. "That word doesn't appear in their writings very often. It usually means 'child,' but…" She found what she was looking for. "It's been theorized that it could have a broader meaning. That is, Kaufman suggested in some of his studies that it could mean any sort of child-like trait, depending on the context." Part of her disliked giving Kaufman credit for anything, but she couldn't deny him proper acknowledgement for his work.

Dieter's eyes narrowed in thought as he read over her translation again. "It seems to say that whoever has been purified must be a child, but perhaps it means to point toward a specific trait of children, as you said. Then it says that it must be one who knows and has followed the gods, and who will show them proper deference and respect." His face lit with an 'aha' moment. "Humble. That's what the word means in this context. Whoever has been purified and considered worthy by the community to use the gem must be humble and respectful of their gods."

Gina reviewed the translation. "That's all it says? Nothing about any traps?"

"Not that I see." He eyed the tunnel ahead. "They may have meant to record it as simple fact, much like the written version of the legend we found before. A written record of their laws."

Lettie took one more picture. "So they just wanted their people to know they had to, like, make their gods happy if they wanted to get the ruby?"

Gina stared at her, brain running through connections. "The Mevoyan culture didn't quite have the same bloody tradition of sacrifices as other native groups in this area, but they did believe in symbolic sacrifices to appease their gods. Perhaps they were required to present a sacrifice at this point."

"Their sacrifices were usually public affairs," Dieter said. He glanced around the narrowing tunnel. "There isn't much room for spectacle here."

"But the priests would have been heavily involved in this process. The person seeking to access the ruby could have given a sacrificial item to the priest overseeing his progress," Gina said.

"So what's that mean for us?" Burke asked, sounding impatient.

Gina drew a blank. She looked around. "The sacrifice might have been a small amount of meat, or a flowering branch. Or it might have involved cutting one's own hand or arm and offering a small amount of blood."

"And?" Burke pressed.

She kept looking but saw no indication of an altar for the sacrifice.

"Maybe the priest wouldn't let the guy pass until he gave the sacrifice," Lettie said. "So maybe it doesn't really matter for us now."

Dieter frowned, his eyes once again narrowed in thought, but he offered no opinion.

Gina checked the ceiling and floor, but still saw no signs of anything relating to Mevoyan sacrificial practices. "I guess that could be." She peered at the cobblestone under their feet. "Savion, do you see anything in the floor? Any pressure plates we should watch for?"

Savion lifted his light to examine the floor in the narrower tunnel space ahead. "No. Not that I see." He paused. "It is difficult to tell."

Gina eyed the tiles. "All right. Let's keep moving." She returned the journal and notebook to her pack.

Will stepped into the narrower section.

"Get down!" Dieter barked out.

Will glanced back, a confused look on his face.

Dieter pushed free of Burke and shoved past Gina and Lettie, launching himself forward before the others could respond. He slammed into Will.

In the same moment, the space of the tunnel filled with spikes.

# Chapter 12

Lettie shrieked as dust billowed, clouding the tunnel.

Gina gasped, backpedaling a couple of steps. "Will!"

A muffled cough came from the mess, sounding close to the floor. "We're okay."

Gina crouched, shining her lantern into the space. The spears and lances left a two-foot gap at the floor. Will and Dieter lay flat in that space, one of the lances nearly grazing Dieter's shoulder.

Savion dropped to one knee and easily pulled Will free, then Dieter.

Will stood and brushed himself off. Dust covered his clothes and streaked his face and hair, caking a small scratch along his cheek. "Nice save, mate. How'd you know?"

Dieter shook his head, sending more dust cascading to the ground. "It was the part about respecting the gods."

"But we didn't see anywhere for a sacrifice," Lettie said, looking around again.

"They had a particular way of showing their deference before their gods."

Gina stared, seeing what he was getting at. "But there are no markings to indicate this is a sanctuary."

"They would have considered it as one, given the power they believed the ruby to hold."

"What are you guys talking about?" Burke demanded.

"Entry into the sacred spaces, or sanctuaries, required prostrating oneself before the gods," Gina explained. "They often would even pass through the entry while remaining prostrate."

Lettie's eyes widened as she studied the tunnel with the spikes filling most of the space. "If someone went in flat, like you said, they wouldn't get killed."

"But if someone disrespected the gods by walking in upright, they would be killed." Gina closed her eyes. She'd blown it again, and almost gotten Will killed. "I'm sorry, Will. I should've thought of that."

Will brushed dust out of his hair, managing to streak more across his face in the process. "No harm done, in the end."

"Thanks to you," Lettie said to Dieter. She smiled and helped him to his feet. "That really was a good catch."

Gina found herself pulling Lettie's arm away from him before she was consciously aware of what she was doing.

Lettie gave her a wounded look. "What?"

Dieter's dispassionate gaze rested on Gina.

She looked away. "It was a good catch." Her mind buzzed through uncertainty, fear, and doubt. That was the second time Dieter had gone out of his way to save Will's life, this time even putting his own life in danger. Maybe she'd had the wrong idea about him. Maybe he really was on their side after all. Maybe she was just jealous that he'd spotted what she hadn't.

Cold reality slapped the thoughts aside. He'd killed Owen and Jake and who knows how many other people. He was a monster. She couldn't afford to let her guard down.

Lettie was looking at her funny now. Gina shook her head and forced her attention back to the tunnel ahead. "I guess we'll have to crawl through to continue."

Thankfully, the others accepted her change of topic and turned their attention toward progressing forward. Even snake-crawling on their bellies, there wasn't enough clearance for them to get through with their packs on. Will took his pack off, set it on the floor, and pushed it ahead of himself as he began wiggling through. Lettie followed in the same manner.

Gina set her pack down, then glanced back at the others. "You aren't going to…" Her eyes flicked to Dieter's tied hands.

"It will not keep him from crawling," Savion said.

She felt some relief. They wouldn't untie him. A pang of guilt followed. It wasn't like he'd be able to try much in such cramped quarters with Burke and Savion guarding him. And after he'd saved Will's life, didn't he deserve a little kindness?

She again shoved the thoughts aside. No. They couldn't afford to give an inch.

Gina turned back to the tunnel and gauged the clear area. "Savion, will you be able to fit okay?"

"I will fit. Go. We will follow."

She nodded and slid flat on her stomach to crawl ahead. Her aching muscles renewed their more vocal protests at the new style of movement, but she gritted her teeth and pressed onward. Burke griped behind her about not wanting to be in front of Dieter, but his voice quieted after an unintelligible rumble from Savion.

Dust and dirt coated the floor, but her pack thankfully cleared much of it from reaching her face. Her arms were another story, and her fingernails turned black before long. Her shoulders and sides itched where dust worked its way under her shirt. She pushed on. It couldn't be too long, right? The entryways were sometimes lengthy to prove devotion, but she'd never heard of one longer than a few yards.

On the other hand, access to the ruby would have required a lot of devotion. She hadn't gotten a good enough look to see how long this part of the tunnel went. Would they have to crawl the rest of the way to the ruby? She winced at the thought.

Hands lifted her pack away, then Will and Lettie were helping her into the space on the other side of the spike-filled tunnel. It was a rounded room, almost teardrop shaped. It widened here where the entry tunnel ended, then narrowed at the other end into the continuing tunnel.

"Thanks." She stepped aside and brushed herself off, eyeing the darkness ahead. Great. More tunnels.

Savion slid out next, pushing his and Dieter's packs ahead of him. He declined Will and Lettie's offers of help. Gina noted that she'd been right to wonder—the bottommost lances came within centimeters of Savion's back. He easily pulled himself clear, then crouched and waited. A moment later, he reached in and hauled Dieter free. Burke struggled his way clear shortly behind Dieter.

"Should we take a minute to rest?" Will asked. He checked the GPS. "We should probably eat something."

Gina looked at the tunnel ahead, feeling a longing that crowded out the other conflicting emotions she'd been suffering. If this was the entry to the place where the ruby was kept, they had to be close. It could be just around the corner. "Can't we—"

"Eat," Lettie said, giving Gina a look that was meant to be fierce.

Gina sighed and sat down, a light cloud of dust rising around her at the movement. Visions of hot showers danced through her head as she dug out some food. She brushed them off. Once they had the ruby and found their way safely out of these caves, it would be the first thing on her list.

After dealing with Dieter. She stuffed a nearly tasteless chunk of protein bar into her mouth to distract herself. She didn't want to think about that right now. For the moment, she just wanted to focus on finding the ruby. She'd deal with what had to come afterwards once they reached that point.

A loud sigh from Lettie broke the silence. "Once we get out of here, I'm never touching another protein bar for the rest of my life. Ever."

Gina couldn't help but smile. "Same here."

"Or freeze-dried crap," Burke supplied.

"What?" Will asked, downing his last bite. "I think they're pretty good."

"Compared to what?" Burke asked.

Will shrugged and took a swig from his water bottle.

Gina finished and pulled her pack on, eager to get moving. "Let's get going. We have to be close."

"If it's really there," Burke said.

"Even if it isn't exactly at the pool, it won't be far," Gina replied, unwilling to let his wet blanket dampen her enthusiasm. After all the things that had gone horribly wrong so far on this trip, she was determined to find the one thing that would start things going right. "We're going to find it."

Lettie scrambled to her feet, her own enthusiasm growing. "You really think we're close?"

"That's the entry. We must be almost there."

Savion untied Dieter and handed him his pack. Once it was back on, the large man tied Dieter's hands once more. "Continue."

Will shouldered his own pack and faced the tunnel. "Nothing we need to watch for here, right? I'm not going to get tackled again, am I?" He glanced back at Gina with a slight teasing smile.

She pulled out her books and checked the notes. "We need to avoid any water sources."

"I thought this thing was supposed to be in a pool," Burke said.

"Yes, but don't touch the water itself. It might be poisoned."

He rolled his eyes. "I wasn't planning on drinking it."

"According to the writings, just touching it can cause madness."

He laughed. "The same writings that said we'd find a siren in there?"

Gina frowned, but he had a point. The pool had to have some sort of fresh source. Otherwise, it would dry up or turn into sludge over the centuries. Even if the

Mevoyans had poisoned the water back when they built this cave system, the poison might have passed from the system in the years since.

"Just be careful," she finally said. "When we find the pool, don't touch the water until we've had a chance to examine the area."

Burke rolled his eyes but said nothing else.

Gina nodded to Will. "It should be safe. Just keep an eye open for any new writings."

He gave her a little salute and continued onward.

The new tunnel was almost as narrow as the one before. Lettie started out walking beside Gina, but soon had to settle for walking behind her, peering over her shoulder to see ahead.

Gina's brain kept grinding away, mentally going over translations and images. Had she missed something? She didn't exactly have the best track record so far. She didn't want to neglect something and get someone else killed. Again.

A renewed pang of guilt prodded at her, but it, along with the fears and doubts, faded at the sight of a faint glow ahead.

"I see light," Will reported, confirming her hopes. "Looks like a pretty big room up there."

"See anything dangerous?" Burke called from the far end of the marching order.

"Not yet."

Gina squinted ahead. They had to still be deep underground. Where did all the light come from?

Will seemed to be moving faster, and she realized she was, too, her body eagerly responding to the promise of a break from the oppressive ink that had surrounded them for so long. As they neared the end of the tunnel, she began to see the space ahead more clearly. From what she could tell, it was massive. The light shone from glimmering veins set in the walls of the space.

"Phosphorescent," Will said. He reached up and turned his headlamp off. The walls ahead seemed to glow all the brighter in response.

Gina quickly turned her own light off, her heart pounding. This had to be it.

As the other lights behind her flickered off, the glow ahead strengthened, filling the space with a bluish shimmer. She could barely breathe, anticipation tightening her muscles and pushing her onward ever faster.

They reached the end of the tunnel. Stepped into the cavern.

Lettie gasped in wonder.

Gina would have done the same, but her body wouldn't respond or do anything but gaze, awe-struck, at the towering space before her.

It was massive, extending several stories up and nearly as broad as a football field. The walls glistened and shimmered with rainbow tones, reflecting and refracting the blue-toned glow from the phosphorescent rocks. It was like standing in the middle of a natural cathedral, just as breathtaking and just as inspiring of reverence and wonder.

Her gaze turned to the floor. She pressed a hand over her mouth, scarcely able to believe what she saw. A massive pool filled a sunken hole in the center of the room. Here and there, lower stones formed ledges along the edge of the still water. Only the faintest traces of light from above reached the surface, creating faint, almost eerie reflections. The faint whisper of moving water was the only sound, muted by layers of rocks and hinting at a source spring further underground.

And a broken, ancient Spanish caravel protruded from the surface. The *Corredor*.

The ship looked like it had been broken into at least two pieces. The aft end rose from the water at an angle near the middle of the pool, the back tilted upwards out of the water and the rest vanishing beneath the surface. Only a few feet of deck were visible from the angle, but the edges they could see were all made of raw, broken boards. Halfway between the aft and the edge of the pool was the only other portion of the ship above the water's surface, all jagged board and broken mast, with the battered remains of the wheel near the middle of it. It was as if the bow had been driven into the bed of the pool, leaving only a small section from the middle protruding upward. Deep water separated the two sections.

The legends had been right. The Spanish ship had been returned to the resting place of the ruby. It was here.

"We found it," she finally managed to say. "We really found it!" She took a step forward.

The ground shook with a too-familiar rumble.

"Get down," Dieter yelled. "Get out of the tunnel!"

Hands shoved Gina from behind, and she found herself flat on the bouncing rock floor. She cringed and covered her head, curling up to protect her body. Was the cavern going to collapse on them? Thunder sounded all around them, filling her ears and muting all other noise.

Then silence.

She hazarded a peek. New clouds of dust lazily drifted down over them. She coughed and waved her hand to clear the air in front of her face. The cavern hadn't collapsed. She turned to check the pool, but only a slight ripple disturbed the surface. The ship hadn't moved. Nothing was damaged there.

She turned back to the tunnel. Rocks filled the space, sealing it off. Sealing them in.

"Hey!" Burke jumped to his feet. He rushed to the pile of rocks and shoved at the nearest one. It wouldn't budge.

Lettie looked around. "We're trapped!"

Gina eyed the walls. There were no obvious exits, but there had to be one. "This whole place has been one hidden passage after another. We'll find something."

"You're sure?" Lettie asked.

"Perhaps an exit will appear after we locate the gem," Savion said.

Will seemed clueless, and Burke still frowned. Lettie, however, seemed content with that answer. She dusted herself off and pointed to the ship. "That's where it is, right?" Her voice echoed through the chamber. "So let's get it!"

Will grinned and started toward the pool, Lettie at his side. Even Savion and Burke seemed on the verge of cracking smiles at the thought of finally reaching the gem.

Gina held back. "Don't touch the water, remember?"

Burke rolled his eyes. "Not that again."

She gave him a look. "The writings say the water could be toxic. And if this is normal, harmless water, then how is it the ship is still here? That wood should've rotted to nothing by now."

Burke didn't have an answer for that.

"I've got it." Will dug into his pack and produced a small device. "It'll tell us if the water is safe."

Burke snorted, but Gina nodded. Better to check, just in case.

Lettie followed Will to the side of the hole, standing above one of the ledges. He dropped his pack on the upper edge and sat down, ready to jump down onto the ledge.

"Hold on," Gina said, visions of the ledges in the purification tunnel springing to mind. She was letting her excitement over the ruby get in the way of the need for caution. She looked around, but saw no writing on the walls, so she dug out her books to check the notes.

"It does not move," Savion said.

She looked up at him. "What?"

He had crossed to the side of the pool, leaving Dieter with Burke. He crouched, studying the ledges. "None of them move. It is safe."

"You're sure?" Lettie asked.

He stared at her. Gina read his expression easily enough. He wouldn't have said it if he wasn't certain.

The look apparently went right over Lettie's head. "Well?"

"He's sure," Gina said. "It's safe." She returned her attention to her books. Might as well double-check, just to be sure she hadn't missed anything.

Will hopped down onto the ledge. Only his shoulders and head were visible from where Gina sat. He vanished from sight briefly as he scooped up a sample of the water.

Gina switched from checking each note to skimming over them, eager to join the others. She knew most of them by heart, anyway.

Lettie shrieked.

Gina's pulse spiked. She looked up, searching for danger. "What? What happened?"

The others stared at Lettie, equally startled.

Lettie pointed to the water. "I saw something move!"

"It's your imagination," Burke said. "There couldn't be anything alive in there."

"I saw it," Lettie insisted.

Gina put her books away and stood, peering at the water. It looked perfectly tranquil, though the dim lighting made it impossible to see beneath the surface.

Will leaned closer to the water. "I didn't see anything."

Frowning, Gina set her pack down. She started toward the others by the water, but glanced back at Burke and Dieter, just to be sure he was still secure.

Dieter hadn't moved. A smirk rested on his face as he watched the others.

Her heart jumped. He knew something. He'd put something together, something she'd missed.

"Get away from the water," she said, her voice louder and sharper than she'd intended.

The command echoed and re-echoed, filling the space with chaotic sound. Savion frowned at her. Lettie and Will looked up, startled. Will took a step back from the water's edge.

Gina remained still, her narrowed eyes searching the space. What had she missed? What was it that Dieter had seen?

"What?" Lettie demanded, her hands on her hips. "You just about gave me a heart at—"

"Shh." Gina took a few cautious steps forward, studied the walls. The broken ship. The pool.

Her eyes widened. She glanced back at Dieter. His smirk grew, confirming her fears.

"Don't touch the water. Don't even go near it," she ordered, hurrying toward the pool. She remained up on the higher ground, peering down at the still waters, but she saw nothing.

"What is it?" Will asked, his expression almost comically blank.

Savion's eyes had narrowed. He, too, studied the pool. "You don't think…"

"The siren." Gina crouched beside the edge and peered down. The water remained stubbornly unmoved. No sign of what lurked beneath the surface.

"That's what this is about?" Burke snorted. "Come on. You really think there's something still alive in there? After how many centuries?"

"The lizards were still alive," Will pointed out.

Burke rolled his eyes. "Great. So what, some pretty lady's going to come out of the water and sing at us now?"

Gina ignored his snide tone. "Lettie saw something. We have to be careful until we know for sure what it was."

"It was a hyper-active imagination," Burke insisted. "I'll prove it." He picked up a loose pebble and chucked it at the water.

"No, don't!" Gina cried, but it was too late. The pebble vanished beneath the surface, setting off a single perfect ripple that spread across the stillness.

No one moved. All eyes were fixed on the pool.

Nothing happened.

Burke grinned. "See? The danger's expired." He snickered at his own words.

A new ripple appeared.

Gina jumped back, staring at the surface with wide eyes. "Did you see that?"

No one answered.

"She's still in there," Dieter said into Gina's ear.

# Chapter 13

ina flew backwards, almost falling over her feet in getting away from Dieter. He watched with mild amusement.

It took a few seconds to get her heartbeat back under control. She leveled a finger at him. "You stay back."

He raised his bound hands and flicked his fingers in a dismissive way. "I was merely examining the situation. Caution will be required. Hundreds of years spent in silence, stillness. I'm quite sure the creature hungers."

"Like you?" she retorted, then caught herself. He was trying to pull her into some sort of game. She couldn't allow that. "Get back over by the tunnel and stay put."

He shrugged but obeyed. He sat on one of the larger fallen rocks and watched, his eyes as intense as ever.

Gina turned her back on him. "Burke, keep an eye on him. Will, can we reach the ship without touching the water?" She dredged up everything she had learned about the *Corredor*. The ruby would have been stored in the captain's cabin, just beneath deck in the aft section. It looked like that part might still be above surface and safe to reach. "It would most likely be in the aft section. Can we get to that?"

Burke gave her a scowl, but dutifully took his post next to Dieter.

Will jumped up onto their level and walked the circumference of the pool. "I could rig up some ropes here," he said from behind and to the right of the aft section, "but it's so far from the edge, we're gonna get pretty close to the water. I can't guarantee we'll stay out of it."

"No good."

"Here," Savion said, pointing from the ledge he stood above. It was just off the front corner of the middle section.

Will skittered over to the larger man's side and studied the area. "Right. We can reach the mast from here fairly easily by running a rope from here to the ship. Then we can form a similar connection to the aft end."

"Let's do that. And don't touch the water," Gina reminded them.

Will returned to his pack and dug out several ropes, looping them over his shoulders, and a handful of metal climbing pegs. He and Savion set to work preparing the line between the edge and the middle section of the ship. Lettie hovered over them, occasionally bouncing from one foot to the other in anticipation.

Gina examined the surface of the pool until she was certain there was no further movement from beneath the water. She glanced back to check on Burke and Dieter again.

Burke looked bored and annoyed. Dieter still looked vaguely amused.

Gina frowned. Was there something else she'd missed? Something she'd forgotten? She racked her mind, thinking back through everything they'd found so far. The still pool of death. The siren. Some sort of toxin in the water. Blood… something about blood? It drew the siren, that's what it was. Good thing no one was bleeding.

She glanced back at him once more, but his expression hadn't changed. That didn't help her feel any better.

Something beeped. Will returned to his pack and picked up the water testing device. "Well, it's not pure water, but there are no known toxins in it."

"What's that supposed to mean?" Burke demanded, stepping forward. He paused and gave Gina a look. "With your consent, your highness?"

Lettie folded her arms. "There's no need to be rude."

"I'll come to you," Will said quickly. He crossed to Burke's side and showed him the device. "It isn't detecting any of the known toxins it screens for, but there's something in the water the system doesn't recognize. I can't say for sure if it's safe or not."

"Better not to touch anyway," Gina said. "With that thing in the water."

Savion straightened from the pins, now secure in the rock floor by the edge. "It is ready."

Will left the device with Burke and returned to Savion's side. He picked up one end of the rope, looped it, and lassoed the mast. The loop caught on a broken board that rested crossways on the mast, probably once part of the sail system. Will gave the rope a tug. It wobbled.

"Not the most secure," he reported. "No worries. I'll get across and get it fixed. Won't be a minute."

Gina stepped closer. "But if it isn't secure, how will you get across?"

He grinned at her. "I got this."

Before she could voice further concerns, he jumped up on top of the rope and walked it like a tightrope walker, arms barely lifted from his sides for balance. He reached the other side in a flash and shimmied down the mast onto the deck. The old boards creaked and groaned, but they held strong.

He flashed an 'I told you so' grin Gina's direction, then reached above his head, pulled the rope free, and set to work re-securing it.

"Circus monkey freak," Burke muttered from behind her.

She gave him a frown and used the opportunity to check Dieter. He hadn't moved from his seat, watching Will as if finding the whole thing entertaining. At least he was cooperating.

Once the rope was in place, Savion looked around. "Who will cross?"

"We shouldn't have too many people over there," Gina said. "I don't know how much weight those old boards will handle."

"I want to go," Lettie said.

Gina surveyed the others. Either Savion or Burke needed to stay on this side to guard Dieter. She'd rather have Savion watching him, but she doubted Burke would be much help in retrieving the gem. Savion's strength would come in handy if anyone slipped while on the ancient deck. But Savion was massive. She doubted the deck would handle much extra weight with him on it. Savion, Will, and Lettie would probably max out the capacity.

She exhaled. She'd wanted to go across herself, but maybe this was for the best. The thought of dangling above the dangerous water sent chills down her spine, anyway. She didn't want a repeat of the climbing adventure getting down the caves. It seemed like so long ago now.

"Okay," she finally said. "Lettie, you cross next, then Savion. I'll stay here and help guide as needed." And watch for the creature. The water still hadn't shown any further signs of disturbance, but she knew it still lurked there.

After they both deposited their packs on the upper ledge, Savion helped Lettie onto the ledge below. The rope slanted upward, making harnesses more of a hassle than a help, so they would be crossing hand-over-hand. The distance wasn't too far. Still, anxiety built in Gina's chest, and she had to focus to keep from picking at hangnails.

"Keep your legs tucked up close," Will said. "Make sure you don't touch the water."

Lettie nodded and set off, dutifully curling her body upward. Her shoes dangled a foot above the surface. Will held onto the mast and stretched an arm out toward her, ready to help her onto the deck.

Gina held her breath the entire time, but Lettie made it across without an issue. She grinned as Will helped her climb higher on the slanting deck, out of the way so Savion could cross. "I made it!"

"Good job," Gina said, scanning the surface again.

Savion tested the rope, sagging his weight against it. It remained firm. Satisfied, he stepped off the ledge, keeping his legs up and away from the water as much as possible, though his bulk left his feet closer to the water than Lettie's had been.

He was about halfway there when the rope groaned. He paused. The mast creaked and shifted an inch. The rope swung downward.

Lettie gasped.

"Hang on," Will said, bracing the mast.

Savion's shoe dipped into the water before he had a chance to react. He quickly curled his body higher, away from the water.

The water churned beneath him. Lettie shrieked.

Then the water was still.

Savion clung to the rope, watching the opaque surface beneath him. No one moved.

Finally, Gina let out the breath she'd been holding. "It's safe. It looks like it won't leave the water."

The large man watched the water a moment longer, then cautiously resumed climbing. The mast didn't move again, and he reached the deck without further incident. The boards let out a chorus of protests under his weight, and he held tight to the rope until he was sure the deck wouldn't break.

Now that all three of them were safely across, Will turned his attention to the other side. "Hmm."

"What?" Gina asked.

"This isn't going to work. There's nothing to catch a rope on over there. And there isn't enough clearance above the water. That end is too close to the surface."

Disappointment and fear rattled through her system. Had they come all this way only to fail now? There had to be another way. She shook the feelings off and studied the layout. "How else could we get there?"

Will was already scrutinizing the area around him. "There are a lot of loose boards and bits here. We could jury-rig a sort of bridge. It wouldn't be strong, but it might be enough."

"Good. Try it."

Savion and Will set to work collecting pieces for a rough sort of bridge.

Lettie made a genuine effort to be helpful, trying to lift pieces that were too big for her and mostly getting in the guys' way. "I found a good one!" she reported cheerfully, tugging at a length of broken railing.

The other end snapped free. She shrieked as the whole chunk of lumber swung into her, knocking her toward the water.

"Lettie!" Gina cried.

Savion caught Lettie's arm and pulled her to safety. Lettie huddled against him, whimpering and shaking.

"Is she okay?" Gina called.

Lettie mutely shook her head.

Will stepped closer and examined her. "She's got a pretty bad gash where it caught her arm."

Gina looked around helplessly. Lettie was too upset to cross the rope by herself. Someone would have to cross. And between her and Burke, Burke was the one who would know how to tend the wound best.

Savion seemed to have the same thoughts. "Burke can cross. The deck will hold."

Gina looked over at Burke. She'd have to stay on this side. With Dieter.

She shuddered but nodded. "Where's the other rock axe?"

"By my pack," Savion replied.

She retrieved it and clutched it close, ready to use it as a weapon if needed. "Okay. Burke, only take what you need to take care of Lettie. The deck won't stand too much extra weight."

He made a show of digging through his pack to find a smaller medical kit, then headed for the rope. "I know, I know. Don't touch the water or the boogeyman will get me."

Rather than responding to Burke's sarcasm, Gina eyed Dieter. "Don't move an inch. Not a muscle, got it?" She did her best to sound brave and intimidating. She had a feeling she'd failed on both counts.

He remained relaxed in his seated position, watching Burke cross to the ship. "I wouldn't dream of it."

It didn't take long for Burke to clean and treat the injury.

"You might as well stay here and help, since you're on this side anyway," Will said, putting a piece of lumber in Burke's hands.

"I'm just here for medical care."

Savion narrowed his eyes at the man. "You will help."

"Fine, whatever."

"I can help," Lettie offered, seeming to have recovered from her near miss.

"Maybe you'd feel better watching from back on solid ground," Will suggested.

"No, I'm okay here."

An awkward look crossed his face, as if unsure how to tell her that her help was less than helpful.

"It is fine," Savion said. He picked up two pieces of board and held them together for Will to secure. "Work."

Burke bickered and griped from time to time, but the three men managed to piece together a rough bridge. Will scampered to the top of the mast and held a guide rope to keep the makeshift bridge off the water as they extended it to the aft section. It clunked against the jagged wood and finally found a secure position, lodged in the railing.

"Monkey, get going," Burke said, pointing to the bridge.

Lettie elbowed him, a severe look on her face.

Will didn't seem to mind, though. He slid back down the mast with ease and stepped on the end of the planks.

"Wait," Gina called. "Tie a rope around his waist. If anything happens, we'll have to pull him back fast."

"Good idea," Will said, smiling at her.

Savion dug out another length of rope and secured it around Will's waist.

Gina eyed their position. She couldn't see the bridge very well from where she stood guarding Dieter. But if she had a better view, she might be able to help guide them. She might be able to see any danger before they did if she stood on one of the side ledges.

She glanced at Dieter.

He raised his hands in innocence. "Not a muscle."

Less than satisfied but lacking much choice, she nodded and hurried to the side of the pool and climbed down onto one of the ledges. She had a great view from there. Enough to see that the end of the bridge wasn't quite as secure as it had looked.

"You need to try to move the end over a little more," she called to them. "It's going to slide off to the right."

Will and Savion pushed at the bridge, working at it until it was properly secure.

"Okay." Gina gestured for Will to go ahead. "Just be careful."

Will stepped out onto the bridge. The planks groaned against the ropes holding them together, but they barely dipped more than a few inches under his expert feet. He was across in moments.

"It's not very stable," he warned as he untied the rope from his waist and set it back on the bridge for them to pull across. "I wouldn't trust too much weight on it."

Lettie glanced at Burke, then Savion. "Guess that's me."

"Just take it slow," Gina cautioned. She glanced over at Dieter. To her surprise, he'd followed her directions and stayed put. His amused expression was gone, though, and he watched with intensity. He wanted the gem as badly as they did.

Lettie allowed Savion to tie the rope around her waist, then she cautiously took a step onto the bridge. It immediately groaned. She gasped and stepped back.

"It's okay," Will coaxed. "It'll move some, but you'll get across all right."

Lettie steeled herself, then slowly started forward. The ropes inched along the planks, but held, only swaying downward an inch or so with each step.

A few splinters dropped into the water.

"Stop!" Gina barked. Lettie froze.

The water churned beneath her.

Lettie gasped and nearly lost her balance. She dropped flat on the planks, clinging to the surface. The ropes slid further. The bridge was going to fall apart.

"Pull her back! Get her back!" Gina shouted.

Savion and Burke pulled on the rope, but Lettie wouldn't let go of the bridge. She stared at the churning water beneath her, frozen in terror.

"Lettie! Let go! Go back!" Will urged.

Burke pulled harder. "Come on! Get off your butt!"

The water churned faster. The creature knew they were there. It knew what was coming.

Gina's heart pounded. She couldn't breathe. The bridge would break. Lettie would fall in. And they'd be helpless to do anything but watch.

Dieter was staring at her. Those intense eyes.

Blood.

The thought whispered through her mind. The creature was drawn to blood.

The bridge creaked and dropped another two inches.

"Lettie! Let go!" Burke howled.

Gina looked down at the ragged hangnails on her fingers. Her bad habit of chewing on them. Without thinking, she chomped on the edge of her thumb until she tasted copper, then plunged her hand into the water.

The churning stopped. A ripple shot toward her.

She yanked her hand back out.

Fingers brushed the surface from beneath. Gina remained frozen, staring as the fingers vanished. And were replaced by a face. The face of a beautiful woman, looking at her with longing and hunger and betrayal. Wondering where the blood had gone.

The siren.

A loud splash tore Gina's attention back to the others. The planks of the bridge vanished into the water.

"Lettie!" she gasped.

"We have her." Savion held the sobbing girl. "She is safe."

Gina nearly fell back against the wall ledge in relief, but quickly looked back down at the water. The siren hadn't emerged from the pool before, but would it come after her now that it had scented her blood? She peered at the dark, glassy surface, but the siren had vanished.

The others were talking, but she couldn't make out what they were saying. Her gaze searched the rest of the pool, seeking out any trace of a ripple or stirring or any other clue to the creature's location.

"Gina!"

She looked up, startled. The others were staring at her.

"We've been calling your name," Lettie said. She'd recovered her own footing, no longer clinging to the men. "What's wrong with you?"

"I saw it." The words burst out before she could stop them.

They stared at her, uncomprehending.

"It—the creature?" Savion finally asked.

Lettie's eyes went round. "What did it look like?"

A shudder slipped down Gina's spine at the image burned too clearly in her mind. The female face. It looked so human, but not quite. Something was off about it. Something that left her feeling cold and empty inside.

Gina pushed the disturbing feelings aside with a wave of her hand. They needed to focus on their goal now. "Will, the ruby should be in the captain's cabin just beneath you. Find a way in that keeps you clear of the water. The rest of you, we need a way to get him back across."

Will scurried around the tilted deck and vanished on the far side of the hull. Burke went back to his usual contentiousness as Savion and Lettie poked around at the remaining planks, trying to find some combination that would be long enough.

Gina found her attention continually drawn back to the water.

"We need more rope," Savion called.

His voice tore her back to reality. She climbed up onto floor level and went to Will's pack. One last coil of rope remained. "This is all we've got," she warned, preparing to toss it.

Burke put a hand up. "Hang on, then. Maybe you should bring it across if it's the last rope. I don't want it hitting the side and falling in the water."

"She can throw just fine." Lettie planted her hands on her hips again and frowned at Burke.

"Across this distance? This is the last rope—we can't risk anything happening."

Gina spoke before Lettie could offer further protest. "It's fine. I'll cross." She didn't want to admit it, but Burke had a good point. She'd always been better with books than anything athletic.

She dropped off her own pack and crossed to the other step. The taut rope dipped and jerked in her hands before she'd even put her weight on it. Her heart dipped and jerked in response.

"It is solid," Savion said. "Cross."

She took a deep breath, but she couldn't coax her legs into movement. Who was she kidding? She hadn't been able to cross a rope like this over the crevasse, and she'd had a harness to keep her secure that time. She was too much of a wimp, too chicken for this sort of thing. She wasn't like Lettie. She didn't want to be Lara Croft or Indiana Jones. She couldn't do this.

"You can do it," Lettie called.

"She's gonna wimp out again," Burke grunted.

Gina's cheeks burned. Will needed her. If she didn't get this rope across, he'd be stuck, trapped on the other side with no way to get back to safety. She had to do this.

She held her breath and curled her legs upward, letting her weight hang on the rope. It sank downward several inches but stopped before her feet touched the ledge beneath her. The rope would keep her high enough to stay out of the water. She'd be safe.

Gina fought the urge to close her eyes and scream. Instead, she clenched her teeth and started forward, hand over hand. The rope shifted slightly in rhythm with her movements, and it took everything in her to keep moving forward. Eyes ahead. Breathe in, breathe out.

Her gaze slid downward against her will. The water remained perfectly still beneath her.

Her hands stopped. Something about it seemed to call to her. Pull her down. The rope dipped lower and lower, obeying the water's call to deposit her, to hand her over—

"Gina!" Lettie's voice pierced the air.

She blinked and looked up. The rope was taut. She still dangled well above the surface.

"What's wrong?" Burke demanded. "Why'd you stop?"

Her mouth was dry. She swallowed with effort. "Nothing. I thought I saw something." Her arms shook, and she had to force them to resume moving. She was already halfway there. And they needed her. Will needed her.

Before she realized how far she'd reached, Savion caught her on the other side and helped her find her footing on the wooden deck.

"Here." She shoved the rope into Burke's hands. "Let's finish this and get out of here."

Savion didn't let go of her. He had a strange look on his face.

"What?" she demanded, still trying to stop her body from shaking.

He slowly released his grip. "It is best that we leave soon," he said, turning his back on her and joining Burke.

Lettie edged closer to Gina. "Are you okay?"

"Fine." Her voice came out clipped, but she didn't bother trying to soften it. Savion was right. The sooner they got away from this water, the safer they all would be.

"I got it!"

They all turned as Will reappeared off the side of the aft. He was covered in grime, but the dirt didn't tarnish his grin. He found his footing on the rail and held out a massive red gem.

The Ruby of Ages.

Lettie took a step back, her eyes widening further than seemed possible. "It's beautiful!" Her voice was barely a whisper.

Burke grinned. "We're gonna be rich."

Savion said nothing, but his face softened at the sight of his people's treasure.

A soft splash came from behind Gina. She spun to see a ripple in the water, but no signs of what had fallen in. Or of the creature. She checked Dieter, but he still hadn't moved. His eyes were fixed on the gem. The hunger in his eyes was almost identical to what she'd seen in the siren's face.

She forced herself to turn back around. Eyes forward. No point in letting him distract her from their victory. They'd found what they were looking for. Now they just had to make their way out of there.

But no hidden passages opened, no new tunnels formed to show them the way out. The way they'd come was still solidly blocked.

She wasn't the only one to notice. "Nothing's changed," Lettie said, panic edging her voice. "We're still trapped!"

"Something will change soon." Gina willed herself to believe her own words. "There's an exit here. We just haven't found it yet. For now, let's get Will back across."

Her words pulled the rest back to their tasks. Will peeled off his shirt and used it to secure the gem while the men resumed work on the new bridge, collecting the planks near the mast so they had plenty of space to build. There were fewer long planks now, so they had to use several shorter planks. Less secure.

Will can make it, she told herself. She leaned against the wheel, near the higher edge of the deck. He'll be fine.

She eyed the water, checking again for any ripples or signs of the siren. Nothing. For some reason, she felt no relief at the thought. The tension in her chest built as her gaze remained fixed on the pool below. Everything around her seemed to tilt as the cool liquid called out to her, whispering, drawing her toward it. A tiny voice in her head screeched at her that she was moving, but she couldn't stop herself.

A hand gripped her shoulder.

Lettie screamed. Burke and Will yelled. Savion crouched, braced to attack.

Dieter's fingers dug into her shoulder, his eyes like black ice. Part of the ropes that had bound him still hung from his wrist, the ends snapped and frayed.

Her entire body trembled. "What are you doing?" Her voice shook as badly as her body. How had he gotten over here so fast? How did he get past the others without anyone seeing?

His eyes seemed to evaluate her for a moment, then he smiled. The smile was more terrifying than his hold on her. "I'm afraid you have forgotten the key translation."

"Let her go!" Burke demanded, crouching like Savion.

"Spring at me if you will," Dieter said indifferently. "The momentum will carry us both into the water."

Burke paused, then slowly straightened. Savion remained crouched.

Gina, meanwhile, racked her brain and came up empty. "It said the creature is drawn to blood. That's all."

His smile returned. "Not that translation."

She stared at him, fear choking her thoughts.

"Think hard. I'm certain you will recall."

Burke growled at the condescending tone, but Gina searched her mind. A cold feeling washed over her.

"It's not literal," she whispered.

"Just as the siren was not literal?"

"They only said that to scare away treasure hunters," she insisted.

He chuckled.

Burke scowled at them. "What are you talking about? What did it say?"

"Tell them."

Gina once again found it difficult to swallow. "It was back in the dome room. One of the texts said that none may leave until the pool looks as blood."

"None may leave?" Lettie's eyes remained large as she looked around. "That's why the tunnel collapsed!"

Savion's eyes hardened. "Until the pool looks as blood?"

"What's that supposed to mean?" Burke demanded.

"I'm afraid I didn't translate it as well as I should have. A better translation would be, 'fills with blood,'" Dieter murmured. He grabbed Gina's hand and lifted her thumb, studying the bloody spot. "I might have normally called you an ideal candidate, seeing how you've already offered yourself to the siren. But there may still be traps ahead, and we'll need your translation skills. It will have to be one of the others." His gaze flicked in Burke's direction.

Burke's eyes narrowed. "Don't even think about it, freak."

"This isn't right," Gina pressed. "We can't—"

"Exactly," Dieter said, his voice as calm as ever. "You can't. I believe you've misunderstood my intentions. Someone has to die. Until this pool fills with blood, we'll never leave. But of course none of you are capable of making that happen. I'm merely volunteering to deal with the more unpleasant part of this endeavor. To do what none of you could. You merely have to select which of you it will be." He looked at Burke again. "I can offer my recommendations, but it will have to be your decision in the end."

Savion lunged. Dieter dropped Gina's hand and caught the man's face, slamming him flat onto the deck. Savion didn't try to get up, panting and glaring at Dieter.

"We're not giving anyone to the siren," Lettie said as firmly as she could manage with a trembling voice.

"Of course not. There would not be enough blood left to fill the pool." Dieter's fingers dug harder into Gina's shoulder as he pulled her a step away from the edge of the boat, turning her to face the others. "Perhaps you should be the one to decide. This is your expedition, after all."

Gina dug at his fingers and squirmed, trying to break free from his grip. "Please, don't do this."

"It's not a choice. I'm merely making your job easier. None of you have to get your hands dirty." He stepped forward to stand between her and the others. "Now, whose blood will fill the pool?"

"We'll give it your blood!" Burke yelled. He charged. Dieter deflected his attack as easily as Savion's. What he wasn't expecting was Savion to move at the same time. The larger man lashed at Dieter's feet, making him stumble. His grip loosened.

Gina tore free and scrambled away from him, her heart thudding painfully with every step.

Dieter growled as he straightened. "There is no choice." His voice remained disturbingly calm. "One must die." His gaze returned to Gina.

She stumbled another step backwards, away from him. She could see it now, the animal behind his eyes, and it terrified her.

Her foot slipped. She gasped and caught the railing to regain her balance.

Dieter's eyes narrowed as if something had gone wrong.

"Stay away from her!" Burke shouted, lunging at him again.

Savion swung at the same time.

Gina's feet tried to move backwards again, away from the fight, but she caught herself in time and glanced back to check her footing. She stood at the edge of the deck. Her gaze flew to the water as if drawn by a magnet. It tugged at her once more, rising up to grasp her and suck her into the depths. The cavern swayed.

"Gina!" Will shouted as she fell.

# Chapter 14

Savion was helpless to do anything but watch in horror as Gina tumbled into the water. He pushed past Dieter, ignoring the shapeshifter's narrowed eyes. He stopped at the edge, clutching the rail and peering over.

Gina surfaced, coughing.

"Get out of there!" Burke shouted from Savion's side. "Hurry!"

A ripple shot across the water from behind the aft. Straight to Gina.

She vanished.

"No!" Lettie screeched. She dashed to the edge, clutching what was left of the rail there. "Help her!"

Burke whirled on Dieter. "I'll kill you!"

The water churned. Gina's head emerged once more. Savion's heart stilled at the sight of long, white fingers gripping the woman's hair. Pulling her back to the water.

Will jumped over the side, holding onto the railing with one hand and reaching the other out to her. "Grab on!"

She gasped in air. Her arms flailed wildly, thrashing at the surface.

"Get her out of there!" Lettie cried.

Gina disappeared beneath the water again. The ripples slowed, then stilled.

Burke's face twisted in fury. He spun to Dieter. "Grab him!"

Savion turned. For once, Burke had the right idea.

Dieter shoved past him and dove into the water.

Lettie shrieked. "What's he doing? What's happening?"

Will remained perched on the hull, squinting at the water. "I can't tell!"

The water churned and became violent, splashing harder until Will had to scramble back onto the ship to avoid getting drenched. Lettie and Burke drew back from the edge, but Savion remained perched at the side, ready to move. Droplets sprayed against his pants, but he remained still, his eyes searching the roiling surface.

The water settled. Lapped. Stilled. The lights reflected red from the surface.

"Blood," Will whispered.

Dieter broke the surface and swam to the step Gina had stood on earlier.

Savion's hand tightened into a fist.

Dieter seemed to struggle for a moment, then climbed free of the water. Gina's limp form lay in his arms.

"Gina!" Lettie gasped.

Savion was already moving. He crossed the rope even faster than before, no longer caring whether his shoes touched the water. On the other side, he leapt onto the floor level and dashed to meet Dieter. He could hear Burke behind him and Lettie squawking from the rope.

Dieter placed Gina on the upper ledge and jumped up beside her.

Savion reached to push Dieter aside. The man caught his arm by the sleeve and snarled at him. For a brief moment, Savion saw the monster's true form.

But then it was gone. Dieter shoved Savion's arm back and turned his attention to Gina's still body.

Savion almost reached for him again. He stopped at a faint tingling sensation in his arm from the damp spot on his sleeve. Something wasn't right.

Dieter adjusted Gina's head and pushed on her chest. Water trickled out between her blue lips, but she still didn't move. Didn't breathe.

Burke arrived, puffing. He reached for her, but Dieter swatted his arm aside.

"The venom is all over her. Do not touch."

"What are you talking about?" Burke shouted. He suddenly shifted his feet, bracing to lunge. "Stay away from her!"

Savion caught the younger man before he could attack. Something told him that Dieter spoke true. Gina herself had said the water could be poisonous, and now it covered both her and Dieter. Burke protested and fought to break free of the grip, but Savion held tight. Lettie stumbled to join them, clutching at Savion's free arm.

Dieter pushed Gina's chest again. More water. More silence.

"Come on, Gina," Lettie whimpered.

The next push brought a larger rush of water. Gina twitched. Coughed.

Savion exhaled in relief.

After several more coughs, her breathing steadied. Color slowly returned to her face. But she didn't wake.

Dieter was silent for a long moment, then gathered her up once more and stood. "And now, if my gracious captors will find a proper camp?" He glanced at the few supplies they still had. "So much as can be found."

Burke shoved Savion's hand away. Savion allowed it this time.

"Not until you tell us what's going on," Burke demanded, standing with his arms crossed in what he apparently believed was an intimidating stance. "Why did you save her after all that crap you were saying about killing one of us? And why won't you let us touch her? I'm the one with medical training, not you!"

Dieter's eyes narrowed. Savion caught a glimpse of the monster again, but as before, it was gone before he could get a good look.

"Feel free to touch her all you like. Enjoy the poison."

"But you can touch her," Lettie pressed.

"I am not affected as you are."

A rumbling sound shook the cavern. Rocks tumbled away from the other end of the cavern, creating an exit.

Savion looked back at the pool. Blood stained the entire surface red.

"What's going on?" Burke demanded.

Dieter's eyes fixed on Savion.

"The pool looks as blood." He avoided the monster's gaze. "Filled with blood. The siren's blood."

"But why?" Lettie tried again. "You said one of us had to die, but then you saved her! Why would you do that?"

Dieter kept his gaze on Savion.

He wasn't as clever as Gina, though. He thought he understood part of it, but the rest was a mystery. He shook his head.

"Of course you know," Dieter scolded, sounding impatient. "Every one of you heard her say where the siren nests."

Savion exhaled. Of course.

"Quit playing games!" Burke thundered. He looked ready to try attacking again. "What are you talking about?"

"The siren nests beneath the pool," Savion said. His voice sounded dull even to his own ears. "It would have killed her in its cave. No blood to fill the pool."

Burke folded his arms. "So why'd you put yourself at risk fighting it and saving her? You could've just killed one of us instead."

Lettie gasped.

"Well, he could've," Burke said, giving her a look.

"The siren's blood was sufficient."

"Then why not kill the siren in the first place?" Burke pushed. "You were the one insisting it had to be one of us."

Dieter's gaze flicked toward the blood-stained water. Savion could have sworn he saw a flicker of regret cross that gaze.

A moment passed before Dieter answered. "Dealing with the siren was not… ideal." With that, he turned and walked toward the new exit.

Savion turned to follow, his mind still working. He'd seen Dieter's eyes narrow, the shift in his expression when Gina fell into the water. The monster had originally intended to kill one of them to fill the pool. But when Gina fell, he'd had to change tactics. Dieter needed Gina if he wanted to escape any further traps. So Dieter had changed his plan and killed the siren, saving the essential translator and filling the pool with blood, as the trap required. Cold. Calculating.

Lettie trailed behind at a distance. "You said we couldn't touch her because of the venom. Is that why she won't wake up? Will it kill her?"

Dieter didn't slow. "Why would I waste time saving her if the venom would kill her?"

"Hey!" Will called.

Everyone but Dieter turned back to see him waving from the railing of the aft.

"I'm still here, remember?"

Savion sighed again. "Burke, Lettie, help him get across. Collect the packs and join us quickly."

Burke's scowled at Savion. "Who made you the boss? First Gina, now you!"

Savion straightened and put on his face, the face he reserved for only the most desperate situations. The fearsome face. The tribal face. "Go. Now."

Burke's mouth closed. He turned and walked back to the pool, Lettie at his side.

When Savion turned back, Dieter smirked at him. He deliberately ignored it and passed the monster, walking through the newly-formed exit to examine the space on the other side. It was another teardrop-shaped room, large enough for them to rest until Gina recovered. "Put her down and move back. You will not touch her again."

★ ★ ★

Gina woke to find Lettie beside her. She tried to sit up but couldn't move. "Wha…"

"You're awake!" Lettie all but screeched in her face. "Hey, she's awake!"

In moments, Savion, Burke, and Will crowded over her.

"How do you feel? Are you hurt?" Burke demanded.

"I can't move." Her words came out slurred.

"It's the siren venom," Lettie said, her eyes solemn. "Dieter said it causes paralysis."

Dieter? He'd tried to kill her. Gina struggled against her uncooperative limbs, but nothing worked. "What happened?"

"He killed the siren and saved you," Burke said. "I guess even monsters can do the right thing. When it suits them."

Confusion clouded Gina's thoughts. Killed the siren? Saved her? Her eyes met Savion's, and suddenly she understood. "The blood." The siren wouldn't have left enough of her blood to fill the pool.

"It worked. An exit opened up shortly after he killed it," Lettie supplied.

Gina closed her eyes. But why had he saved her, especially if he knew that she'd be paralyzed? She couldn't be any help to him in this state.

"Let her rest."

Dieter's voice sent a chill through her body. Where was he? She couldn't see him from her position.

Burke and Will backed off. Savion and Lettie lingered. As Burke and Will sat down near the walls of the rounded room, Gina saw Dieter lounging on the far side of the space. His hands were tied once more. Her teeth clenched. Not that it mattered, apparently. He would snap the ropes again when it suited him to do so.

"Just relax," Lettie said. "He said it'll take some time for the venom to wear off, then you'll be able to move again."

So she could still be of use to him. She wanted to grab Lettie's arm, but her limbs still wouldn't respond. "Listen to me! You can't trust him," she whispered. "Don't let him out of your sight."

Lettie's eyes widened. "He saved your life, Gina. He didn't have to do that, you know. He could've let you drown after he killed the siren."

"Only because he still might need me for translating."

"He saved Will too," Lettie pressed, shaking her head. "Maybe he just did it because it was the right thing to do."

"He doesn't know the definition of the right thing to do." Gina met Savion's eyes and saw understanding there. She relaxed. He would keep his eyes on Dieter. He would make sure they stayed safe.

The others rested quietly while waiting for the venom to wear off. Will snored soundly, leaning against the rock wall as if it was a comfy hammock, and Lettie dozed off and on. Burke remained awake, though his drooping eyelids proved him as exhausted as the others. Even Savion, sitting ramrod upright with gaze fixed on Dieter, looked like he'd sleep for days given the chance.

Dieter was the only one who didn't seem affected by the lengthy, grueling expedition. He looked almost bored.

Gina tried to focus on moving, eager for the paralysis to wear off. She felt too vulnerable, lying on her sleeping bag and unable to move. If Dieter decided to try anything, she'd be unable to defend herself.

He wouldn't, she reassured herself. He's practical, if it can be put in such terms. She still might have use to her, so he wouldn't try to kill her. Yet.

She exhaled. Once they found the exit to the caves, they couldn't wait for any sort of formal justice or authority to deal with Dieter. They'd have to kill him before he could turn on them. Savion and Burke would be her best allies in that cause. She was fairly certain Savion would have come to the same conclusion on his own, but it wouldn't hurt to talk to him privately and confirm they were on the same page. Maybe she could sneak aside with him and Burke to make sure they'd be ready when the time came.

Her plotting kept her awake and occupied until she finally felt a strange tingle in her fingers and toes that gradually spread up her limbs. It was like the pins and needles from sitting too long in one position. She shuddered and gasped in joy when her arms and legs responded to the conscious movement.

Will and Lettie woke at the sound. Burke blinked his eyes open from the light snooze he'd slipped into. He glanced at Savion and Dieter, then crossed to Gina's side. "Can you move?"

She wiggled her toes and fingers and almost cheered again. "I think so."

Her arms and legs were a bit less responsive as Burke helped her sit and shone a light in her eyes, but they improved quickly as he went through the paces of a quick physical exam.

"Looks okay," he finally said. "We can get out of this deathtrap whenever you're ready."

She flexed her fingers again. "I think it'll be better from here to the end. They would have been more concerned about people getting in than getting out."

Burke snorted. "Because they thought people can't use the exit as a way in?"

"They would have placed the exit somewhere very difficult to reach and well-hidden. It's fairly normal to Mevoyan customs that there'll be other traps to keep people from coming in that way which won't affect people walking out."

Burke raised an eyebrow.

Will tilted his head, looking similarly puzzled. "How would that work?"

"Kaufman found a sacred temple once, about seventy miles from this area. The way in was filled with traps and puzzles, but the way back out was smooth and easy, just a stone-paved, downward path. They marked the hidden exit so they could use that as their entrance. But when they returned and tried to come back in that way, they couldn't. The paving stones had been cut so that one edge, the downward one, was razor sharp. Climbing down meant skipping right past the danger, but climbing up faced nothing but the sharp edges. They had to go back through the long way again."

"So you think we'll find sharp-edged rocks ahead?" Will asked.

"Possibly, or some other sort of trap which only allows passage one way." She pulled out her journal and leafed through it. Her air-dried sleeve moved stiffly over her arm, making her itch. She absently scratched the spot while she studied the writings. "There aren't any notes about any special traps or things to get through after the ruby's pool, so I'm pretty sure we should be fairly safe from here, as long as we keep an eye out for any other writings."

"Or any other trouble," Burke muttered, giving Dieter the stink eye.

Dieter acted like he didn't notice.

Will shouldered his pack and offered Gina a hand. "If you're ready, we can work on getting out of here."

Lettie joined in helping Gina stand.

Her arms and legs wobbled, and for a moment she was unsure that she'd be able to stay upright when they let go. She probably would be better off if she waited and rested a little longer, but she wanted out of these caves. Away from sirens and falling rocks and spikes hidden around every corner. And done with Dieter.

The thought brought back her nausea, and she turned away from it, reaching for her pack. "Yeah. Let's get going."

Lettie helped her roll her sleeping bag and secure it to the pack. Gina almost couldn't lift the pack, but she gritted her teeth and muscled through it.

Will gave her one last glance. "You sure you're ready?" His tone suggested he felt the same as her, eager to move on and leave the cave far behind.

She nodded.

He looked relieved. "Great. Let's go."

The tunnel leading out of the space looked just like all the tunnels before. Cobblestone floor. Natural rock walls only occasional shaped by tools to keep the tunnel a relatively consistent size. Gina was glad for the monotony, since she had to divide her attention between watching for signs of Mevoyan writing and keeping her weakened legs moving in a straight line.

They'd only gone a few steps into the tunnel when she froze. In all the panic over her paralysis and the threat Dieter posed, she'd completely forgotten the most important thing. "The ruby! Did we get it?"

Will glanced back with a slight grin.

Lettie giggled and squeezed Gina's arm.

Savion slung his leather pack free and dug inside. He gently lifted out a huge, cloth-wrapped object.

Gina could barely breathe.

He set his pack down and unwrapped the cloth. First a glint of red showed, then a side, and then the last corner of cloth fell free.

The Ruby of Ages.

Gina reached out with shaking hands and touched it, too awe-struck to speak. It was as massive as the legends said. And beautiful. The Mevoyan people had left it in its natural form, believing that shaping a sacred item like this could defile its spirit. As such, it had a crystalline appearance, with several natural facets, each one glinting pomegranate red in the LED lights.

"This is really it," she whispered.

Lettie's eyes crinkled further, though she remained quiet, seeming to understand the reverence of the moment.

Will gazed at the gem with a sideways grin, the joy of discovery on his face.

Dieter seemed mesmerized, that same hunger once again in his eyes.

Gina felt suddenly cold.

"Let's get going," Burke said, his tone sharp. He must have seen the look on Dieter's face, too.

Savion carefully re-wrapped the gem and returned it to his pack.

Gina felt the cold feeling dissipate back into delight. They'd found it. They'd actually found it! The fabled ruby would be put on display in a museum for people from all over the world to admire. The forgotten Mevoyan people would be known across the globe. And Kaufman could take his smug attitude and stick it.

She couldn't help but grin as they resumed walking. The whole place felt lighter than before, no longer seeming quite so dark and oppressive. Or maybe that was her own feelings of elation.

Lettie squeezed her arm again. "I can't believe we really did it! It was just like Lara Croft." She paused. "I think those spikes were the same as a trap in one of her games, too."

Gina shook her head and chuckled. "Sure."

"Hey," Will said. "Check it out."

The tunnel ahead split into two branches. One went steeply downward, deeper into blackness. The other angled just as steeply upward.

Lettie squinted at the upward tunnel. "Is that—do I see light?"

"Daylight?" Gina asked, almost afraid to hope.

Will clicked his headlamp off. "Looks like it." He grinned. "It's the way out."

Gina wanted to cry. Finally, they were free.

"Wait."

Savion's quiet command splashed ice water over Gina's excitement.

Burke scowled at the larger man. "What? We found the way out. You want to stay in this craptastic place, feel free. The rest of us are out of here."

"Do you think there's a trap?" Gina shone her light at the walls and ceiling around the tunnels but saw no markings or writing. The cobblestone pattern looked the same as always, but he'd been able to see the traps in the floor before. "Is there a stone we shouldn't step on?"

His eyes flicked back and forth between the tunnels. "We must go down."

"That's deeper in the cave," Will said. "We have to go up to get out."

"Like I said," Burke added before stepping toward the upward tunnel.

"Hang on." Gina put up a hand, slowing Burke. She turned to Savion. "Why do you think we need to go down?"

He remained silent a moment longer before speaking. She thought she heard a trace of hesitation in his voice. "There is an old saying among my people. 'If you wish great heights, you must first accept the depths.' I have long thought it merely a metaphor for humility. But here…" He looked at the two tunnels again. "I believe the lower tunnel is the only safe one."

"This is stupid," Burke pressed.

Will looked up at the faint glow of daylight at the apex of the tunnel leading up. "But you don't see any pressure plates on the floor."

"No."

"And there's nothing written on the walls," Will continued.

"I haven't seen anything," Gina said.

"And nothing in your books?"

"No."

Will shone his light down the other tunnel, then returned to the upward tunnel. "That's the way to the surface. Every danger so far has been marked by a lever, a pressure plate, or writing. If we aren't seeing any of those, then we have to assume it's safe." He stepped into the tunnel.

"Finally, some sense." Burke gestured for Savion to follow Will.

Savion didn't move.

"Come on," Burke pressed. "Don't you think your people would've left something more than just an old proverb for something this important?"

"Look, it's perfectly safe," Will said. He took a few more steps further in.

"Maybe we should check out the other tunnel," Gina said, uncertain what to think. Will and Burke had a point—so far, every trap had possessed some physical sign of its presence, even if it was just a pressure plate in the ground. But if Savion was right, they'd be walking straight into danger.

"Don't be silly." Will took a few more steps and waved his arms around. "There's nothing here."

Dieter sniffed, frowning at the tunnel.

Lettie glanced at Gina. "It looks safe. He's still okay. Maybe it really is the way out."

Burke stepped into the tunnel, then folded his arms and glared at Savion. "Would you come on already?"

Will sighed. "Look, I… I know you hired me to get you through this place. It's been a real trip, way freakier than the stuff I usually go through. Which is cool in its own way and all, but I'm ready be done with it, you know? If you want to come back and check out that lower tunnel later, I'm cool with that, but for now, I gotta get topside. Sorry." He turned and steadily hiked upward.

Burke pointed. "Let's go."

Savion still didn't move, watching Will with hard eyes.

Dieter sniffed again. "Will, come back."

Will ignored him and kept walking.

"Not you, too," Burke groaned.

Dieter stepped forward, pushing Burke aside. "Get back down. There's something in the tunnel."

Will coughed.

Gina's heart jolted. "Will?"

He coughed again, then doubled over in a wheezing, hacking fit.

Lettie stepped back away from the tunnel, pressing a hand over her mouth. "What is it? What's wrong with him?"

Dieter held his breath and hurried to Will's side. He grabbed the younger man's arm and pulled him back toward the group. Will kept choking and coughing, his hands pressed over his face and body bent over. His legs buckled as his coughing faded into weak gasps. Dieter dragged him the rest of the way free of the tunnel, depositing the skinny man on the floor and dropping against the wall to suck in air.

Burke crouched and rolled Will on his back.

Blood ran from Will's eyes, nose, mouth, and ears. His eyes remained open, but no longer saw.

Lettie gasped. Gina clenched her teeth against a sudden rush of bile.

Will was dead.

# Chapter 15

Gina's already-weak legs gave out, depositing her on the floor.

Lettie sank down beside her.

Burke straightened slowly and looked up at the lighter tunnel. Shock, disappointment, and anger flashed across his face in succession. He glared at Dieter. "How did you know? Why didn't you warn him earlier?"

Dieter stood straight, eyeing the corpse at his feet. "I failed to detect the gas until he'd already inhaled it."

"Gas?" Lettie squeaked.

"I'm not familiar with this specific type," Dieter said. "I only noticed an odd odor at first. I didn't realize it was dangerous until it was too late." He looked up the tunnel. "It must be a lighter gas, like helium, causing it to be trapped around the apex of the tunnel."

Burke's angry gaze shifted to Savion. "You knew."

"Back off," Gina said, finding her voice. She was recovering faster now, as if she was getting used to seeing so much death around her. Becoming numb to it. She doubted that said anything good about her, but she didn't have time worry about that now. "He tried to warn Will not to go that way."

Burke's jaw muscles twitched for a moment. "Fine. We'll take the other tunnel. Let's get moving before we all end up dead."

"We can't just leave him like this," Lettie whispered. She seemed to be recovering faster, too.

"Forget him. He was too dumb not to walk right into a trap. I want out of here," Burke snapped.

Anger flared through Gina's system. "You were about to walk right after him, so you have no ground to stand on. Now shut up and help us."

Burke seemed more subdued as he helped tend to the body. They didn't have much to work with in the bare, stone environment, but finally settled on caring for the body as best they could and covering him with his sleeping bag. Burke and Savion moved supplies from Will's pack into their own bags.

"We'll come back if we can, get him a proper…" Lettie's voice broke. "Daddy's going to build them all a memorial. A really big one."

Gina squeezed her friend's hand and turned away from the shrouded corpse. "Let's go."

Savion took the GPS and led the way into the deeper tunnel. The darkness seemed to grow and press in against the edges of their lights. The weakness still gripping Gina's muscles joined forces with the numbness invading her mind, making her steps drag and her thoughts slow. She struggled to stay alert, to watch for writing or levers or signs of danger, but she couldn't focus for more than a minute at a time before the bleak murk around them dragged her back into the soul-numb state.

Lettie clung to her arm, shining her own light around in increasingly anxious ways. Burke and Dieter's lights glowed behind them, but the glow almost seemed to fade the deeper they got in the tunnel. Almost as if the dark around them was a living creature fighting against the invasion of his territory, gradually smothering their lights so it could devour them.

The space around them widened abruptly, then narrowed ahead to resume the march forward in an almost triangular shape. Gina made it a few steps into the space before remembering to check for signs of traps. As she shone her light around, she saw two more tunnels branching away on either side of the tunnel they'd just come from. She shone her light back ahead at the one tunnel in front of them. Her dulled brain finally put it together. It was another branching, like the one they'd had to navigate before, but this time they were coming out instead of in. For them, there was only one path to get out. For someone trying to get it, it would be a labyrinth of false tunnels.

This was how the Mevoyan people had protected the exit from unwanted intruders. She doubted there were written instructions anywhere for this one. It was designed to be impassible from the other direction.

Still, she had Lettie take a few pictures while she made a half-hearted sweep of the area. The thrill of discovery had worn off, replaced by a weariness and longing to be free of these caves, to find sunlight and leave the gloom of death far behind. Finding nothing but bare cave walls, she gestured the group onward.

The darkness pressed in further as they descended deeper. They passed a second branching, then a third. By the time they found the fourth one, she barely paused long enough for a couple of pictures before trudging on. Teams of scholars would thoroughly excavate the site later, led by her warnings of where the traps were. They'd finish cataloguing and recording these tunnels. She might even join them, someday later. Much later.

It became a struggle to put one foot in front of the other, and it consumed all her attention. Something inside her warned that she might miss something important, like a written warning on the wall. Or a painting. Or a tap-dancing monkey. She didn't even care anymore.

Cold air brushed against her cheek. She looked up and realized the tunnel wasn't so oppressive anymore. Or quite so dark. In fact, it now led upward instead of downward. That's why it had become harder to walk.

Lettie blinked as if waking up. It seemed the darkness had cast the same gloom over her. "Is that…"

"I smell it," Burke said, excitement in his tone. "Fresh air!"

"I believe we are near the exit," Savion said.

Gina exhaled, feeling suddenly lighter. Stronger. "We made it."

"I wouldn't make such statements until we have reached our goal," Dieter said.

His voice grated against Gina's nerves. They'd still have to deal with him. She hadn't found her chance to speak with Savion and Burke. Hopefully they'd already drawn the same conclusions she had.

She steeled her will. "I think Savion's right. We're close."

Dieter didn't answer.

The tunnel grew rapidly brighter before it leveled off. Gina kept glancing over her shoulder, feeling more and more certain that Dieter would try something once the exit was in sight. But Burke seemed to be taking his guard task seriously, keeping a close eye on Dieter. Good. That would help when the time came.

The space ahead widened, and they emerged into a massive cavern space. The cobblestones vanished into unaltered cave floor. A dark space dropped off on the far-right edge of the cave, a natural pit of sorts.

Gina wasn't entirely concerned with that part, her eyes fixed ahead. At the far end of the space, the path narrowed once more to twist and wind in a climb upward, weaving between stalagmites and outcroppings of rock. At the top of that climb, daylight streamed in a gentle beam, barely visible from their vantage below.

Her breath caught. Tears threatened her eyes. They'd finally found the exit. They were free.

The last traces of the numbness washed away as her former excitement blossomed. They'd found the ruby and made it back out. They'd done exactly what they'd set out to do. What this meant for the remnants of the Mevoyan people, for the world, for the scientific community, and for her personally… It overwhelmed her. She discovered a smile on her face that wouldn't quit.

"Is it—is that the exit?" Lettie breathed.

Gina blinked back the tears. "That's it."

"Are you sure?" Burke asked. "No more traps? No hidden gas or anything?"

He was right to be skeptical, cautious. Gina shone her light around the space. Lots of stalagmites, paired by stalactites hanging from the ceiling, all in varying shades of grey and brown with the occasional streaks of red. No pressure plates. No levers. No written warnings on the walls. It almost looked like this path had been formed entirely by the elements of nature with no shaping from human hands.

"I don't see anything," she said. "Savion?"

"I believe it is safe."

Her smile returned, wider this time. "We made it."

"You're absolutely sure?" Burke pressed.

"Absolutely," she promised. Poor guy's nerves were getting the best of him. She did her best to reassure him. "Lettie and I will go first, if you want. That's how sure I am that it's safe." She turned to give him a comforting smile.

He didn't return the smile. Instead, he lifted a gun and leveled it at her head.

Gina froze, her eyes wide in shock.

Lettie gave a little squeak, her grip on Gina's arm tightening.

Savion took a step forward, but Burke waved the gun, stopping him.

"You keep back, muscle boy." Burke flicked a glance in Dieter's direction. "You too, freak."

Dieter's expression remained distant, almost aloof. He quietly took a couple of steps back.

Burke eyed him a moment longer. "I've got no quarrel with you. I know you've just been waiting for us to get near the exit so you can make your move. Stay out of my business, and you'll get a nice all-you-can-eat buffet here." He jerked his head toward Savion, Lettie, and Gina. "But if you twitch one muscle in my direction... I've heard all those stories about garlic cloves and silver bullets, but you and I both know that a bullet in the brain will end you just as easily as a normal human."

Dieter's eyes narrowed slightly.

Burke returned his attention to the others. "Now, hand over the ruby."

Gina fumbled for words. "But, but you—how could you?"

"Really?" he asked, condescension dripping from his tone. He screwed up his face and spoke in a mocking falsetto. "We promise not to follow you, and the next time we beat you somewhere important, you aren't allowed in." His voice returned to normal. "Could you make it any more obvious that you were onto something?"

Her heart sank. "Kaufman."

Burke waved the gun again. "I don't see you getting the gem out, muscles. Get moving."

Savion remained still a moment longer, then slowly slid his pack into his hands.

"You're working for Kaufman?" Lettie asked, her tone wounded.

"That's one way to put it. He keeps certain individuals on retainer for when he needs their… expertise."

"Like pretending to help us, only to betray us and take the gem," Gina spat.

"But you can't. Everyone will know what you did when we tell them what happened here," Lettie declared.

Gina almost cringed visibly.

Burke laughed out loud. "You're cute, you know that? I love the naïve ones. I thought you were fun," he dipped his head at Gina, "but you, Barbie, you've been a real barrel."

Lettie blinked, not quite getting it.

"Go on." Burke smirked at Gina. "Explain it, great scholar."

Lettie turned wide eyes on her.

Gina swallowed. "He's going to kill us."

Impossible though it seemed, Lettie's eyes widened further. She stared at Burke. "You can't do that. You—you aren't a killer!"

He laughed even harder at that. "You're right, sweet cheeks. I'm not a killer. I just arrange… accidents. Not to sound cliché or anything." He gestured with his gun, still aimed at Gina. "If I don't see that gem in five seconds, big guy, you're going to have one less translator championing your people."

Gina swallowed. She wanted to move, to step back, to duck away from the gun, but her body wouldn't cooperate.

"I don't understand," Lettie whimpered. "What do you mean, accidents?"

He rolled his eyes. "Accidents. Convenient accidents. Like a rockslide that 'accidentally' crushes a bleeding heart from Kaufman's inner circle who was going to share their findings with their rivals…"

Gina's breath caught. The guy from Kaufman's team who'd tried to meet with her.

"…or those same rivals, caught in a cave-in within feet of the exit." He morphed his face into a mockery of grief. "So tragic, those poor people. I only barely managed to escape with my life myself. But look at that—I found the ruby! Guess it's not a total loss, despite my obvious mourning for my fallen colleagues." He smirked.

"But then Kaufman won't get any credit," Gina said, desperate to stall.

"I said I'm on retainer. I didn't say I'm his lapdog. I know how much that chunk of rock is worth." He eyed Savion. "Speaking of which…" He cocked the gun.

Dieter stepped closer.

Burke swung the gun on him. "I said—"

Savion lunged, swinging his pack. Burke turned and fired. The pack hit his arms at the same time, sending the shot wild and the gun flying. Lettie screamed and dropped into a crouch, covering her head.

Gina dropped, too, but quickly pulled Lettie to the side, away from the men. Her ears rang in the aftermath of the gunshot so badly that she feared she'd lost her hearing for a moment. She shook her head, trying to clear it and focus as the ringing faded. They'd have to make a break for the exit.

Burke slugged Savion and dove for the gun. Savion rushed after him, reaching to tackle him. Burke pivoted, caught Savion's arm, and sent him sailing across the floor. Savion's hands scrambled over the floor to slow his momentum, but it was too late. He vanished over the edge of the pit.

Lettie screamed again.

Dieter suddenly appeared at Gina's side, pulling her to her feet. "Run!"

Burke stopped in the path between them and the exit. Picked up the gun.

"Run!" Dieter repeated, shoving Gina back toward the tunnel they'd come from.

Gina's brain kicked in and finally got an order through to her legs. She bolted, Dieter pulling Lettie just behind her.

Burke shouted. Another gunshot thundered through the cave, momentarily restoring the ringing.

"Your light," Dieter panted behind Gina. He had to repeat it before she heard him clearly. "Turn it off."

They were giving Burke something easy to aim at, their lights showing him right where they were. She fumbled with the lantern hanging from her belt as it bounced madly with every running step.

"Turn it off!"

Her fingers found the power control. The light flicked out. Dieter's was already off.

Lettie sobbed.

Dieter snatched the headlamp off her head and threw it behind them. It shattered against the rock floor.

The tunnel flooded with inky blackness.

# Chapter 16

Gina almost froze in place, but she forced herself to keep moving forward. She had to. Burke was after them, and he had his own light. If he caught up, they were dead.

Dieter's hands touched her back. "Five more feet, then angle right."

She gasped and flinched away from his touch and the reminder that her current company wasn't much safer than the maniac chasing them. She took a shaky breath and forced herself to focus. Dieter was helping them again. She'd have to put up with his presence until they were safe from Burke. Then she'd have to figure out how to deal with him. "How do you know?" She saw nothing but blackness ahead.

His eyes almost appeared luminous, like a cat. "I can see. Only a little, but enough. Angle right."

She shifted her direction, her arms stretched in front of her. The right one touched rock wall.

"Keep going," Dieter hissed. "He isn't far behind us."

Lettie whimpered.

"I can't…" Gina stumbled over an uneven spot. Were they in one of the dummy tunnels? They'd be caught in a trap. She wanted to kick herself. Why hadn't she taken the time to write down the directions as they came through the first time? She hadn't been thinking, that's why.

"We have to move faster," Dieter pressed, frustration edging his voice. "Let me lead. Put your hand on my arm."

Everything in her recoiled from the idea. But another part of her, a more logical part, knew she had no choice. They were going too slow. Burke would catch them.

With Dieter and his night vision leading and guiding them, they could navigate the dark tunnels faster.

Her stomach threatened to rebel, but she searched with a fluttering hand until she found his arm.

He responded with a surge of speed, gradual at first but picking up quickly. Gina heard Lettie's footsteps, almost as clumsy as her own, staggering over the uneven ground. Still, they managed to find their stride and keep up with Dieter.

They turned again after a couple minutes of running, to the left this time. Gina couldn't be sure in the oppressive blackness once more surrounding them, but she had a feeling they'd passed through another hub and were in a new tunnel.

"He's falling behind," Dieter puffed. "I think we're safe to slow down now."

Gina immediately let go of his arm and dropped her hands to her knees, panting. Lettie sounded about in the same shape, only slightly less out of breath in spite of all her personal fitness trainers.

"Keep quiet," Dieter whispered. "He's still searching for us."

Gina tried to slow her breathing and failed. She settled for putting a hand over her mouth, muffling the sound as best as she could.

Footsteps clattered behind them. A faint light bobbed in the darkness.

Gina froze. She couldn't stop her panting before. Now she couldn't breathe at all.

Burke's loud curse echoed through the tunnel, and Lettie whimpered again.

Dieter's breath blew hot near Gina's ear. "We have to sneak further in. He'll hear her."

Gina cringed, flinching away from his nearness. But once again, he was right. She felt in the darkness until she found his arm again.

"Move slow. Try to stay as quiet as possible," he whispered, his voice barely audible over Burke's footsteps and Gina's pounding heart.

Gina's feet hit a rough patch, and she stumbled, her feet thumping on the rock. She winced.

The footsteps behind them grew louder. Faster. He'd heard.

Dieter immediately responded by running again. Gina almost lost her grip on his arm, struggling to keep hold.

"Stay close," he said. "I'm going down a wrong tunnel."

So he'd been taking them down the right path. How had he kept track? Probably because of his… what he was. She shuddered in spite of herself.

He led them through a direction shift, then stopped and shifted his feet to one side. Gina felt his arm brush a wall and realized he was pressing against the side of the tunnel. She started to lean, but stopped, the fear of traps holding her back.

"This wall's clear," he whispered to her. "Stay close to it. He'll pass us by." He moved Lettie back beside Gina, gently pushing both of them flat against the wall before standing behind them, on Gina's other side.

The footsteps neared. The bobbing light.

Gina felt Lettie shift beside her. She instinctively reached over and covered her friend's mouth.

They remained frozen, still. Waiting. Gina's heart pounded even harder now, fear and exertion keeping it thundering in her ears so loud she was sure it would give them away.

The footsteps paused. The light flashed across the mouth of the tunnel they hid in.

Lettie made a faint squeak, muffled by Gina's hand. Gina felt warm tears slide over her fingers from her friend's cheeks. In truth, she felt like crying herself. Or throwing up. Or wetting herself. Maybe all three. Crazy thoughts danced through her head, trying to convince her that Burke would spring at them any moment, that she should just make a sound and get it over with now.

The footsteps moved into the tunnel beside them. The light faded, then vanished, leaving them once again in total darkness.

Gina almost collapsed with relief. Lettie clung to her, shoulders shaking with almost silent tears.

Dieter remained silent and still a moment longer. "He's moved on. We're safe, for now."

"What are we going to do?" Gina whispered.

"Return to the exit. Find our way out and get help." He paused. "You two will have to deal with that part, I'm afraid."

"What about Savion?"

"He most likely was killed in the fall."

Lettie sniffled.

"But we should check," he continued. "If he wasn't, we should do what we can to help him. But Burke won't keep chasing the tunnels for long before he goes back. His goal is to get the gem and leave, trapping us in a cave-in. I'm afraid we've given him a rather good opportunity."

"Then we better leave before he goes back," Gina said.

"He may have already started back. Some of these tunnels wind around and rejoin later hubs."

She stared at him, though she still couldn't actually see him. "How would you know something like that?"

"I took us down one of those. I can hear the echoes through the tunnels and tell where they lead, at least to some degree. That's how I suspected this tunnel was safe."

She exhaled. This was too crazy. She still was having trouble wrapping her mind around the thought that she was actually trusting her life to this guy.

"Can we turn the lights back on now?" Lettie whispered, fear cranking her voice up two pitches.

"Too risky. If he doubles back, he'll spot us. We'll have to be careful and move as quickly as possible without the lights." Frustration edged his tone again. "It's difficult, guiding both of you with…" He paused. "But we'll make do."

Lettie voiced the thought that slipped unwelcome into Gina's mind. "It'd be easier for you if your hands weren't tied, wouldn't it."

"It's not too great a barrier," he said. "I understand why you feel it's necessary. I respect that."

"We could—"

"Lettie, no," Gina said sharply.

"But he's helping us. He saved us from Burke. I think he's on our side."

Gina wanted to cringe at her friend's naïvete. But at the same time, part of her whispered that Lettie had a point. Dieter could have hidden in the tunnels and escaped with ease, unburdened by two functionally blind women. He probably could even climb down that pit without too much difficulty, retrieve the ruby from Savion's pack, and escape before Burke had a chance to get back to the exit. But he'd chosen to stay with them. To help them.

She pushed back against the thoughts, but they persisted. If all he cared about was the ruby, he'd have left them to their fate in a heartbeat. Before, she'd thought he was helping them out of a sense of practicality. He needed her translating skills and Will's ability to navigate. But now Dieter knew where to find both the ruby and the exit. There was no practical reason for Dieter to save their lives. If he really was just a monster, then why help them now? There was no logical reason.

As foolish as it seemed, maybe Lettie was at least partially right. Maybe Dieter really was trying to help them.

"Gina?" Dieter's voice sounded almost concerned.

He was waiting for her to take his arm again. She blushed. She was being silly, wasting time dithering around in her mind after impossible puzzles.

Still, whatever his end game, he was trying to save their lives now. She bit back her doubts and reached for his wrists. "We can move faster if your hands are free."

"Are you certain?" He sounded surprised.

"Don't think this means I'm not keeping an eye on you," she warned. Her hands found the ropes and fumbled blindly at the knots.

"I'll do it." His arm flexed under her hands. The rope snapped.

She flinched back from him, but his hand found hers and took it gently, as if giving her a chance to pull away. Every self-preservative instinct inside her cried for her to do just that, but she told herself that this just proved she was doing the right thing. He could've snapped those ropes at any moment, but he'd chosen to wait until they gave him permission before doing so. She pushed back against her instincts and forced herself to accept his hand. "Let's go."

It was significantly easier with him guiding them more directly. Little adjustments in his wrist told her when to move in closer, when to move faster, when to slow down.

They changed direction. How many turns had they taken to get there? Two that she remembered, but they were running so fast and she'd been so scared, she couldn't be entirely sure.

Dieter's hand flew around her waist and pulled her back against him.

She gasped, turning to push and claw and flail until she was free, but then she heard the soft hiss behind her.

"What is that?" Her voice came out as more of a squeak than she'd intended.

"It's not coming after us. Don't worry." His dodge of the question was less than comforting.

He returned his hand to hers and resumed guiding them forward. The hiss faded into silence behind them.

She shuddered. From the sound of it, she'd almost walked right into whatever it was. Her fingers tightened on Dieter's hand.

Faint light appeared ahead. Daylight. They'd found the exit again. She almost collapsed in relief. It took her a moment to realize this meant she could let go of Dieter's hand now.

"We made it," Lettie breathed.

"Quiet," Dieter cautioned. He sniffed the air.

Gina tensed. "Is he close?"

Dieter remained silent for a moment. "I'm not sure." He picked up the pace, and soon they were back in the larger cavern.

No signs of Burke in the room. Gina exhaled in relief.

Lettie hurried forward. "Come on, let's get out of here!"

"We can't leave Savion," Gina said. She turned on her lantern and held it high as she stepped toward the pit.

Lettie reluctantly followed.

Gina peered down into the pit. It fell deeper than her light would reach, even when she crouched and shone it as low as she could. Various edges stuck out in ledges and jags, but she saw no sign of Savion. Or his pack.

Dieter crouched behind her and squinted. "I can't see him. Turn off your light."

She complied.

He studied the pit a moment longer, then shook his head. "I can't tell." He set his pack on the ground next to the pit. "I'll climb down and see if I can find him. I know you'd rather leave. Go ahead. I'd do the same in your shoes."

Lettie looked as if she wanted to take him up on his offer, casting a longing glance toward the daylight above.

Gina clenched her teeth. She wanted to run, to throw her pack and lantern and anything else that reminded her of this nightmare trip into that pit and bolt for the fresh air and freedom promised above. "I can't."

"Let him have the stupid ruby," Lettie said. "Let's get out of this hellhole!"

"It's not that. I can't leave Savion." He'd been part of their group, one of the few remaining Mevoyan people. She couldn't just walk away from him.

Dieter nodded. "Gather the ropes from the packs. I may need help if I find him." With that, he grabbed the edge of the pit and slid over the side, disappearing into the darkness within moments.

Gina fumbled with her pack straps and got it off her back. "Do you have any rope?"

Lettie paused, then pulled her pack off. "I'm sorry. That was horrible of me."

"No, it wasn't." Gina exhaled. "Maybe a little. But we've been through a lot. It's understandable. I want to make a break for that exit myself."

Lettie gave her a small smile before returning her attention to her bag. "I don't think I have any rope."

"I don't have any, either." She dug into Dieter's pack and found a single coil. "I guess this'll have to do. I just hope it'll be enough." She looked around. Several stalagmites looked strong enough to secure the rope. She glanced over the edge of the pit and felt a slight twinge of nausea. Maybe she should have Lettie do this part.

Stones clattered above them. Lettie gasped.

Burke stepped in through the exit, his gun in hand and a wild look in his eyes. He spotted them before Gina had a chance to pull Lettie back out of sight.

"Where is he?" Burke demanded, pointing the gun back and forth between them in rapid succession. "You're hiding him. Where'd he go?"

Gina's heart thudded painfully against her ribs. She'd been so caught up in rescuing Savion that she'd forgotten Burke could find them at any moment. How'd he gotten outside so fast?

She closed her eyes. Of course. Dieter had warned them that the tunnels could loop back around. Burke had made it back to the cavern before them. She felt like an idiot. Why didn't she think? Why didn't she consider the possibilities before they bit her on the butt?

"Where is he?" Burke repeated, his voice louder, more on edge.

"He went down there," Lettie squeaked, pointing to the pit. "He climbed down."

"Not Dieter!" Burke stumbled around a stalagmite and continued forward, keeping the gun unwavering on them. "Savion? Where are you hiding him?"

Gina glanced back at the pit, lost. "He… he fell in there. You saw it yourself."

"But he's not there anymore, is he?" His tone suggested that he wasn't asking a question so much as stating something they should already know. "And he didn't leave. I checked. No one's walked through that exit in ages. You found him and hid him." His voice pitched upward, his control cracking. "Where is he?"

Gina put her hands up, hoping the gesture would calm Burke down. "We haven't seen him since he fell. Dieter climbed down to find him. If you just wait for a minute, he'll be back with Savion." And the ruby. Or just the ruby, if Savion hadn't survived the fall. She pushed those thoughts back and avoided voicing them.

Burke laughed. It wasn't a controlled laugh like before. It was almost hysterical. "You think I'm sticking around for that monster to get back? I'm gonna have that ruby and be long gone before he gets back up here." His eyes unfocused for a moment, then centered on Gina. "But you don't know where Savion is. Then he's hiding. Which makes my job easy." The gun's barrel lifted an inch toward Gina's forehead, then swung to Lettie's. "I just need to find the right motivation to encourage him to come out."

Lettie cringed, whimpering.

"Please," Gina tried.

"Savion," Burke called in a soft, sing-song tone, ignoring her. "I've got a couple of sweet girls here. They'd really like you to come out of hiding now and show yourself. Because if you don't, I'm going to put some pretty little holes in their pretty little heads."

Lettie gasped on a sob.

Gina's entire body shook. She wasn't sure where she found the strength to speak, but the words came out of her mouth regardless. "If you're really there, Savion, don't come out. He's just going to kill us all anyway."

"Shut up!" Burke thundered before returning to the soft voice. "You don't want to see them hurt, do you, Savion? Come on out before I lose my temper."

"Don't do it!" Gina pressed.

Burke's eyes flashed with rage. He swung the gun and fired.

Lettie jerked and crumpled to the floor.

A ragged cry tore free from Gina's throat. She dropped to her friend's side, hardly noticing the painful ringing in her ears this time.

Lettie clutched her shoulder, trembling with wide, stunned eyes. Blood oozed between her fingers.

Still alive. Gina almost melted, but quickly pulled herself back together. She dug into her pack and pulled out the first cloth item she found, pressing it against the wound in her friend's shoulder. If the movies were to be believed, Lettie would live. Gina hoped they were right.

The barrel of the gun crept into her peripheral vision, and she jumped, cringing away from it without letting go of Lettie.

Burke glared at her a moment longer before speaking in his quiet, sing-song voice again. "Poor, sweet Lettie's hurt awful bad, Savion. And Gina's next." He leveled the gun at Gina's leg. "She's going to hurt a lot."

Lettie trembled. Silent tears snaked down her cheeks.

Her friend was going into shock. Gina looked around in desperation. "Please, Burke. Don't do this."

He smacked the butt of the gun against her temple. Lights flashed in front of her eyes before the ground hit her from the other side. She lay still, gasping for a moment before she was able to fight past the blinding lights and pain in her head. Her hands fumbled. She managed to push herself to a sitting position and press on the cloth over Lettie's wound again. Had to stop the bleeding.

"I'm not playing around, Savion," Burke hissed. His gun remained fixed on Gina. "You get out here before I shoot your little golden girl, too."

# Chapter 17

Gina fought tears, helplessness sinking in. Lettie would die without medical attention. But that was Burke's aim anyway, to leave them all dead in the cave. He'd found them before they could escape, and now it was all over.

Pebbles clattered near the edge of the pit, sending a jolt of adrenaline through her numb mind. Someone was there. Savion? Dieter? Her eyes searched the area, but she saw nothing but the same stalagmites and rock formations, some large, others small.

Burke heard it, too. He spun to face the sound, still keeping the gun trained on her, the aim drifting up toward her chest. "I hear you." He let out a hysterical giggle. "I hear you, Savion. You better show me that ruby before I tear a hole in this sweet little girl."

Silence.

He cocked his gun. "You're trying my patience, big guy. So I'm going to count. You know how counting works, right? They do that in your backwater, inbred little tribe? Five… Four…"

Gina searched the area again, desperate, trying to send her message without words. *Just let him do it. Don't come out and get yourself killed.*

"Three…"

She clenched her teeth, steeling herself.

"Twoooo…"

A blur of movement. Brown fur. Flashing claws and fangs.

Burke screamed as the monster tackled him to the ground. A shot split the air. Gina felt a burning sting through her arm. A cry tore free from her lips as she fell back against the rock floor, but it was drowned out by screams and snarls rising in a discordant cacophony, sharper and louder by the second, echoing in the eerie quiet that followed the deafening gunshot.

Burke's cries cut off mid-scream.

Silence.

The ringing in her ears took longer to fade. Lights still danced in front of her eyes. Maybe she had died after all. The ringing sound was angelic bells. The lights were pearly gates. The angels would come to greet her and find out her halo size. It seemed to be taking a long time, though. And the angels had forgotten to remove the uneven rock floor jutting into her side.

Dieter's face appeared in front of hers. Distinctively human-like. Not angelic. Not a monster, either. He was speaking, but she couldn't make out the words.

He gently picked her up and set her against the wall, sitting upright. Her eyes caught a glimpse of a red mess a few yards from her, and she turned away from it. She didn't want to know what had happened to Burke. He was gone. The threat was over. That was all she cared about.

"Here we are," Dieter said softly, examining her arm. "It's a flesh wound. You're going to be okay." He vanished, then reappeared with a medical kit from his pack. Her hazy brain marveled at his tenderness as he cleaned and bandaged the wound. Her heart sang. He really did care. He wasn't just a monster, there to kill them all. He was her friend. Her study partner. Dieter.

He finished caring for her wound, then gave her a drink of water. "Better?"

She nodded, struggling to find words. "Lettie?"

He gently smoothed her hair back from her forehead and smiled. "I already saw to her. She's going to be okay."

Warmth sank through her system at his words. It really was over now. It was going to be okay.

Dieter straightened and returned to the larger rock formation he'd sprung from behind, reappearing a moment later. He pulled Savion's limp body into the middle of the room.

Gina struggled to sit up, but her body rebelled. "Is… is he…"

"He's alive. Hurt, though. A few broken bones, and he hit his head rather badly." Dieter bound a wound on Savion's leg.

Gina exhaled, surrendering once more to her body's exhaustion. Savion was still alive. He'd survived the fall.

Dieter straightened, brushed his hands off, and retrieved the rope Gina had found. "I'm so sorry you had to go through that. I wanted to move sooner, before either of you were shot, but I was too far away. He'd have killed you both before I could've reached you."

She closed her eyes. She felt like she should be crying again, but her body was too weak and worn for even that. All she wanted now was to sleep, to descend into blissful ignorance, to let this be over. The pain in her arm felt more like a distant numbness now, as if agreeing with the desire for oblivion.

When she opened her eyes again, Dieter was tying Savion's hands together with a length of the rope.

She frowned. "What—" Her voice came out slurred from the pain and numbness weighing down on her.

"Shh," he murmured. He bound Savion's feet, then crossed to her.

"What are you…"

He gently lifted her hands and tied them together, then smoothed her hair back away from her face and kissed her forehead. "It's okay now. Shh."

She tried to protest, to push away from him, but the oblivion creeping in on her was stronger. The last thing she saw was his smile before she passed out.

★ ★ ★

Rushing, crashing sounds invaded the darkness swimming around Gina. A dull ache in her head throbbed in concert with a sharper pain in her arm. She groaned and tried to push away from the sensations.

Something rough scratched at her back. She winced and managed to pry her eyes open. A blast of light forced them shut again. She cringed, then blinked rapidly until her eyes adjusted. Sunlight. She was outdoors.

The smell of saltwater pricked her nose. She squinted as the world finally came into focus. She stood on a beach, leaning back against a tree. A couple other trees stuck out at random from the sand, but there wasn't much space. Steep cliffs surrounded the space, cutting off the small patch of glistening sand from the rest of the world.

It had to be the cave's exit, she realized. Secluded. Hidden. It fit. She tried to turn to confirm it, but she couldn't move more than a couple inches.

She blinked against the last vestiges of haze still fogging her mind. A few rocks jutted from the sand here and there around her. Their packs rested against one of them, the GPS unit clipped on her own. Savion lay on the sand not far from the packs, still unconscious.

Her heart jolted at the sight of his bound hands and feet.

Dieter.

She looked up sharply and was rewarded with a crippling pain in her head. She gasped, struggling to fight back waves of nausea and pain.

"Take it easy." Dieter's voice was quiet, calm. "You've been through a lot."

She managed to pull herself together and open her eyes again. Dieter stood off to the side, ruby in hand. He seemed to be winding some sort of wire around it.

She tried to step away from the tree, to look for a chance to bolt and get away. Again, she couldn't move. The sensations reaching her foggy brain sorted out and began to make sense as she looked up at her arms. Her wrists were bound together and tied to the tree far above her head. Another pair of hands were tied against the tree near hers. She followed them down to find Lettie sagging beside her, blood soaked through a bandage on her shoulder. Her eyes were closed, and her face looked entirely too pale.

Trembling seized Gina's body. "Lettie?"

"Shh, let her sleep," Dieter said softly. "She'll wake soon enough."

The trembling intensified. "What do you want with us?"

He smiled and continued wrapping the ruby. "Did you ever tell campfire stories as a child?"

"What?" She struggled to push the rest of the haze away, to ignore the pain and terror gripping her. She had to get free. To get away.

"Did you ever tell campfire stories? You know, ghost stories and the like."

She glanced at Savion. "Savion? Can you hear me? Wake up," she called.

"I'm guessing you did," Dieter continued. "And you heard the scariest story of all. The Ondier. Monsters that really exist."

Her legs threatened to give out. "Please, Savion, wake up!"

"And if you heard that story, then you heard how they came into this world."

Savion wasn't waking up. She'd have to get the three of them out of there herself.

"You did, didn't you? Hear about how the Ondier came into this world?"

She forced herself to look at Dieter again. Tried to calm her breathing. "Please let us go. You can have the ruby. Just let us go."

"Didn't you?" he pressed.

She'd have to play along, keep him happy until she could find an opportunity to free herself. "Yes, I did."

"Tell it to me."

"Please…" Play along, she reminded herself. Keep him occupied. "There was a giant storm one night, and a window opened in the sky. Hundreds of Ondier came through that window before it closed, and then they spread."

He laughed. "That's a rather dry telling, don't you think? Usually it's much more dramatic, with a lot of artistic flair." He shook his head, adjusting some of the wires around the ruby. "But you've got the essential details, even if you don't have the storytelling flavor."

"What do you want with us?" Her voice came out small.

"And when was this window supposed to have opened?"

"Hundreds of years ago. Long before any of us were around."

His smile widened. "Yes. Hundreds of years ago. Approximately six hundred, to be precise."

Ice flooded her veins.

"Right about the time a Spanish ship set out to finish its expedition. To return home with a great treasure."

She shook her head, words struggling to leave her mouth and failing. What he was suggesting was impossible. They were just legends. They couldn't be true.

And yet words and phrases danced unbidden through her mind. The power of the ruby would shape the oceans. A giant storm. The power of the ruby caused the sky to open.

A window in the sky.

Her body trembled. Her hands twisted, struggling against the bonds holding her. "That's not… it can't be. It's impossible."

He only smiled in response.

She looked around, desperate. "Then you have what you want. You have the ruby. Do whatever you want with it. But let us go. Please. I promise, we won't tell anyone. Not a soul. I swear."

He laughed and admired his handiwork. The wire rose in a loop above the ruby, making it look like a crude, jeweled ring made for a giant's fingers. "Even if I thought you weren't lying through your teeth, I wouldn't do that." His eyes met hers. "And you know why."

She stared, uncomprehending.

An impatient sigh blew past his lips. "Gina, you're far more clever than you give yourself credit for. You know this."

She searched her mind, seeking the answer, the connection she'd missed. The ruby's power. The caves. The…

Her breath caught. Only the pure in heart could use the ruby's power.

Dieter's smile spread as he saw it click. "I'd have been less concerned about you and Savion, but I'm not certain what the exact effect on her will be, given her weakened state. The gem will destroy even a healthy person, as the writings indicated." He glanced at Gina. "My apologies. That was another moment I left out part of the translation. The Mevoyan people didn't kill the fool who used the gem to make the power stop. It stopped on its own after consuming the fool who used it."

He smiled again and turned his gaze to Lettie. "But she's not particularly healthy at the moment and may not last long enough for the gem to do its work. If she's unable to withstand the gem's power, I'll need…" He paused, searching for words. "Backups, if you will."

Gina stared in horror. He was going to kill Lettie. "It's just a legend. Part of the Mevoyan beliefs. They were just concerned about keeping their sacred temple pure."

"Just a legend, hmm? Like the power of the ruby? Like the siren?"

She couldn't answer that.

A distant look passed over his eyes. "It's unfortunate I had to kill that marvelous creature. My people had whispered of its existence for years, and it was humbling to finally see one of my own ancestors in person."

Gina's breath caught.

He glanced her way, the distant look gone. He smirked. "Yes, one of my ancestors. The first ones who passed through the portal back when the 'fool' opened it weren't quite prepared for the trip. The Mevoyan people were able to trap them as guardians for their temples. She was the only one left." He shook his head. "But it couldn't be helped. Regardless, you're correct that the Mevoyan people had their share of myth mixed into what they said about the gem. But one thing I know without question: whoever activates the ruby must have a certain innocence to them. One I most certainly do not possess."

He stepped forward, holding up the wires on the sides of the loop, the ruby hanging down between his hands. Her body shook harder. She saw what it was now.

A necklace.

He gave her one last smile, then stepped past her. He lifted Lettie's head.

Lettie groaned and stirred, but still didn't wake.

"Oh, well. I doubt it's necessary for her to be conscious for this part." He lifted the loop of the necklace above Lettie's head.

"Stop!" Gina's mind raced, frantic for some answer, some way to convince Dieter not to carry out his plan. But she already knew the hopelessness of her situation. She was tied up, trapped, unable to physically stop him. He was going to use Lettie to activate the ruby, and it would open a new portal. Earth would be flooded with Ondier once again. Maybe forever. There was nothing she could possibly say to convince him that letting his people win was a bad idea.

She looked at Lettie's pale face. She couldn't stop this. She couldn't save the world.

But maybe she could save her friend.

"Please, stop. Don't hurt her." The next words stuck in her throat. She swallowed hard and forced them out. "Put it on me."

Dieter's hands stilled. His eyes narrowed, shifting in her direction.

"Please, just leave Lettie alone. Put the necklace on me." Every instinct for self-preservation inside of her screamed at her to shut up, to stop before he changed his mind and did exactly what she was saying. She drew in a shaky breath, fighting to ignore the internal screams. "I'll power the gem."

He looked surprised now. Then his eyes softened. "Greater love," he mused. He let go of Lettie and faced Gina. "Pure in heart, indeed."

Gina cringed. She wanted to beg him not to do this, but she knew it wouldn't make a difference. And he might go back to Lettie if she protested. She clenched her teeth shut tightly and forced herself to stand upright instead of melting into the pool of fear that wanted to swallow her up.

"Well done, my friend." Dieter's smile grew. "This is far more perfect than I ever imagined." He lifted the necklace over her head.

She clenched her eyes shut.

The ruby dropped against her chest. It landed with a soft thud. She expected the weight to drop and drag against her neck, but it seemed to fasten in place against her chest instead. Heat spread across her ribs as a faint glow appeared in the center of the gem.

"Stop! Get it off!" she shrieked, struggling. The ropes bit into her wrist and wouldn't let go. The glow brightened steadily, increasing the heat until it felt like it was burning its way through her chest. She screamed and twisted, but it clung to her body. Her muscles were growing less responsive. The brighter the stone glowed, the weaker she felt, as if it was draining away her very life.

Savion lunged at Dieter, the ropes hanging loose from his outstretched arms. Gina almost cried out in relief. He'd woken up and gotten loose. He would save her.

Dieter caught Savion's arm and flung him aside like a child's toy.

The light burned brighter, beginning to form a beam. Gina cried out in pain as the heat grew searing. She had no strength left to struggle, to do anything but weep, sagging against the tree.

Savion lay gasping on the sand, fresh blood staining his bandages. Dieter stepped toward the fallen man, his fingers twitching. They almost looked like claws for a moment.

A flash of metal appeared in Savion's hand. His throwing knife.

Dieter snorted. Stopped, his hands outstretched as if ready to catch it.

Savion's eyes remained fixed on Dieter, dark with deadly intent. He flung the knife.

Toward Gina.

The blade sliced through the rope binding her hands to the tree. She crumpled to the sand, landing on her side. The beam grew further, stretching toward the sky, sucking the strength from her body.

Had to move. She struggled against the darkness pressing into her vision. She had to get the ruby off her before it could open the portal. Her hands wouldn't respond to her commands at first. The original rope he'd used in the cave still bound her wrists together. She clenched her teeth and struggled to muster her dwindling strength to reach for the gem, to fling the necklace off her.

Her hands found the gem. Pulled.

It didn't budge. She lacked the strength to lift the heavy rock.

Dieter slashed at Savion, but Savion managed to roll aside just in time to dodge the strike. Another blade appeared in his hand.

Gina stared at it, desperate. "Savion," she cried, but her voice didn't work. She fought the weakness around her and tried again. "You have to kill me. Kill me! Before the portal opens!"

His eyes flicked to her, then back to Dieter.

She tried to move, to give him a better target, but her legs wouldn't work anymore. It wouldn't be long before she'd be paralyzed. She had to act, to do something, anything, before that happened.

Dieter stepped closer to Savion, smirking. She realized what he already knew. It wouldn't do any good for Savion to kill her. Dieter would just take the ruby and use it on Lettie. And if anything happened to Lettie, Dieter would use the ruby on Savion. That was the whole reason he'd worked so hard to keep them all alive. Backups, he'd said.

The darkness crept closer. She hardly noticed the pain anymore.

Savion slashed the knife at Dieter's legs.

Dieter easily dodged.

The clouds swirled above as the beam of light reached them.

Dieter's hand flew. Savion tumbled further down the beach, bloody gashes across his chest. He didn't move again.

The crashing waves grew louder. Wilder. The storm was forming.

Gina fought, struggled to push the ruby off. Her fingers barely moved. The gem had drained her. She was helpless to do anything but watch.

Dieter reached her side and pulled her up, back against the tree. Her head lolled. Being careful not to block the beam of light, he lifted her hands above her, to where the rest of the rope still dangled from Savion's knife. "Don't worry. It'll be over soon." He looked back at the reddening sky with a smile as he held her hands with one of his and reached for the loose rope with his other hand.

She had to stop him. If she didn't, if he opened that portal, if the Ondier invaded Earth…

She summoned every last ounce of energy left in her body. Twisted her hands free. Dropped them over his neck.

He turned back, startled. A look of horror crossed his face. "Don't!"

He reached to push her away, but it was too late. With the last of her strength, she pulled him tight against herself, crushing the ruby between their bodies.

They crashed to the sand together. The beam of light snapped back to the ruby, surrounding them with a glow that burned brighter and brighter until Gina had to close her eyes to keep from being blinded.

Dieter screamed, his body writhing and twitching. Even those sounds and sensations faded into the glow. Gina let it take her, swallow her into nothingness.

But it wasn't nothingness.

A bird called in the distance. The waves crashed. The sand felt warm beneath her.

She opened her eyes. She lay on her side in the sand, her hair floating around her in the salty breeze. The ruby lay beside her in the sand. No sign of a glow. No sign of the wires that had once held it.

No sign of Dieter.

She struggled up but could only make it to her hands and knees. The ropes had vanished along with the wires.

Lettie. Savion.

She turned to her friend. Lettie stirred with a faint groan. She still looked pale, but alive. Gina wasn't sure the same could be said for Savion.

She dragged herself to his side. His chest rose and fell in shallow breaths, blood still draining from the gashes on his chest. Not as deep as she'd thought. He might make it if she could get him help.

Her body resisted her efforts to move, but she gritted her teeth and struggled over to the packs. Grabbed the GPS and activated the emergency signal. Found the medical kit.

Gina barely comprehended the next few minutes as she clumsily did her best to bandage Savion's new wounds and press against them, trying to stop the bleeding.

The GPS beeped. Someone had detected the emergency signal. They were coming. Help was on the way.

She sagged against Savion in relief. "Hear that?" she murmured, feeling the heaviness creep over her once more. "We're saved. We made it."

Her eyes roved over the beach and landed on the ruby. It lay in a soft indentation in the sand, simple and unassuming. And very visible.

She closed her eyes as the chopping sound of rescue helicopters rose above the crashing of the waves.

# Chapter 18

Gina brought her Jeep to a stop above the cliffs and climbed out, feeling the salty breeze twist through her hair. She thought with a faint smile that it had a distinctive smell, though she knew in her logical mind that it smelled the same as any saltwater beach. Still, the familiarity of the scent took her back a year.

The site had been scoured by all sorts of scholars and archeologists. The artifacts had been catalogued and moved to museums. Those who'd been lost during the expedition were given proper burials.

Lettie's father had indeed built a memorial—a really big one—for all who'd fallen during the trip. Lettie had seen to that as soon as they returned safely to the States. Last Gina had heard, Lettie was on a trip in Europe to explore her new hobby, hang gliding.

While Savion had avoided the spotlight, Lettie and Gina made sure to share as much of the story as they could with anyone who would ask. It didn't take long for the story to spread, and shortly after that the police found evidence in Burke's ratty apartment linking his work to Kaufman. Last she'd heard, Kaufman was still in his second round of appeals.

She detected a whisper of movement behind her, but she didn't turn. "It's been a long time."

Savion stepped beside her and stared out over the waves. He didn't answer. He didn't need to.

Gina breathed the salty air in and let it out slowly. "I thought this site was never going to quiet down. Every time one group finished their work, another group showed up, wanting to check the place out."

"Still searching for the ruby," Savion said.

"Yeah. Maybe I should've told them Burke accidentally shot and destroyed it."

He shook his head. "They still would have searched for the pieces."

"I suppose." She'd come up with the best story she could, and Lettie had been all too happy to agree on making it the official version of events. They'd found the pool. Even found the *Corredor*. But the ruby had been nowhere in sight. Most likely lost at sea when the *Corredor* wrecked. She'd hoped the suggestion that the gem was beyond reach would dampen others' desire to examine the ruins beyond academic curiosity. She'd underestimated the human lust for discovery. And fame. And fortune.

"Well, things finally quieted down for now," she said, walking toward the relatively new trail carved down to the small, secluded beach area. The height didn't bother her anymore. After what she'd been through, she doubted much of anything would. "But I hear another group's planning on coming in tomorrow or the next day. We're lucky we got this window."

He followed her down to the beach. Her eyes traveled over the sand, the rocks, the trees. The one tree in the middle. She'd have been happy never to see that tree again. But she had to be here today.

She led him to the rocks on the side, the ones their packs had leaned against. The memories flitted about the back of her mind. She was surprised at how little emotion she felt.

Savion knelt beside her at the foot of the rock. They dug into the sand with their hands, deeper and deeper until Gina's fingers felt something hard and rough. Gritty, and not just because of the sand.

"I've got it," she said quietly.

He helped her scoop the sand clear until the red gem appeared. He reached in and carefully lifted it free.

Neither of them spoke for a long moment. Gina finally broke the silence. "It's yours, as far as I'm concerned. Take it back to your people, do whatever you feel should be done with it. Just please—don't sell it. Or put it in a museum. We can't..." She exhaled. "We can't risk another Ondier finding it."

His eyes took in the ruby, then shifted to the ocean. "I liked your story."

She looked at him, question in her eyes.

"Lost at sea." He straightened and tucked the ruby into the bag he'd brought. His eyes scanned the horizon. "It has been a long time since I have sailed. Perhaps it is time for me to take another trip."

Gina nodded. She couldn't help but smile. "I think that's a good idea." She held out her hand to him. "Thank you. For everything."

He met her eyes and shook her hand. But he didn't let go. "Tell me. Do you like to sail?"

She blinked. "I've never gone sailing before."

He paused, then nodded and released her hand.

Her heart beat a little faster with newfound boldness. "But I'd like to learn."

"Ah." Savion reached for her hand once more. A smile crossed his face for the first time. "Then I will have to teach you."

# THE END

# About the Author

I enjoy life with my life-mate and little sprout in the Pacific Northwest. I obtained a degree in Counseling Psychology from Northwest University in Kirkland, WA, which I use to create fully dimensional characters with unique personalities and quirks. In fiction, I'm a huge fan of all things speculative: anything where the rules of reality need not apply. My books include traditional fantasy, space fantasy, post-apocalyptic, and more. When not writing, I can usually be found reading, watching movies, or wasting entirely too much time on the internet.

Connect with me at

cybishop.com